WIDE AWAKE

THE GODDESS CHRONICLES BOOK ONE

K.B. ANNE

GRIPPING TALES, LLC

This is a work of fiction. Names, characters, organizations, places, events, and incidents are either products of the author's imagination or are used fictiously.

Published October 2018
Copyright © 2018 by K.B. ANNE
All rights reserved.

No part of this book may be reproduced or stored in a retrieval system, or transmitted in any form or by any means, electronic, mechanical, photocopying, recording, or otherwise, without express written permission of the publisher.

Published by Gripping Tales, LLC, Pennsylvania.

ISBN: 9781728727974

Cover Design by Anika Willmans, Ravenborn Covers

Editorial Services by Laura Parnum, Laura Parnum Books

❦ Created with Vellum

TO MY READERS,

You are FIERCE.
Don't let anyone tell you otherwise.

> We've all got both light and dark inside us. What matters is the part we choose to act on. That's who we really are.
>
> —Sirious Black to Harry Potter,
>
> J.K. Rowling, Harry Potter and the Order of the Phoenix

THE PROPHECY

One of love, one of light,
Spring forth from the womb
To guard from the night.

The power to heal. The power of youth.
Their existence to all a living proof.

As immortality weighs,
One shall fall, one shall rise,
To perish from all humankind.

CHAPTER 1

*G*litter-Farting Unicorns

I LIE. I cheat. I steal.

Parents don't trust me with their daughters or their sons.

That desk shoved next to the teacher's desk? Mine.

The hint of smoke in the bathroom when you apply your lip gloss? That's me.

The "inappropriate" language scrawled across the fifty-seven million posters advertising the pep rally? You're welcome.

Did you find my use of color on the drawing depicting the mating habits of Kensey and her boyfriend particularly intriguing?

Good. I'm glad we agree. But don't get too comfortable with that bony ass of yours, because if I find you in my seat at the principal's office, I'll wrap my black-tipped daggers around your designer-label shirt and make you realize that after-school detention for skipping class is the least of your worries.

"Freak," you'll mutter to yourself, and you'll be right.

Oh, and by the way, "Skunk Girl?"

One would think the combined efforts of three-quarters of the junior class could serve as one master brain and come up with a nickname a bit more imaginative than "Skunk Girl." Ever hear of Google?

Honestly.

The torture I'm subjected to on a daily basis is un-freak-ing-believable.

"Gigi," Mrs. Kelso whispers, pushing her bowl of fall-themed York Peppermint Patties over to me, "he caught you on film."

I shrug with indifference as I unwrap my orange-foiled mint. It's only a matter of time before they kick me out. The school shouldn't spend so much energy disciplining one troubled youth.

Principal Donahue's door swings open.

Make that two troubled youths.

At Donahue's side stands a shiny new plaything.

Black leather jacket.

Black motorcycle boots.

Ripped jeans.

Tall, muscular body wearing his clothing admirably.

Expulsion becomes the last thing on my mind. For once the rumors are true, and I am front and center to the greatest novelty our school has ever witnessed: the foreign exchange student. Three words packed with the promise of awkward fumblings in janitor's closets without all that pesky long-term commitment business getting in the way.

His steely gray eyes pin me in place like the dead swallowtail butterfly I mounted on cardboard when I was seven.

Together we fall into a cheesy '80s movie scene with sunshine beaming on the drool-worthy specimen while unicorns fart glitter rainbows out of their asses. In a long, drawn-out moment, I imagine all the legendary things we can do together.

Until he opens his mouth.

"You're mine," he says in a deep, husky Irish accent.

The surprise of his voice combined with his words turns my brain into a useless pile of shit. I have no doubt that an extraterrestrial being is about to rip through my chest full-on *Alien* style.

This boy—no, this man—glides across the room and out the door, leaving Mrs. Kelso and me staring at each other like mind-blown idiots. And the hammering in my chest makes me think I'm having a heart attack.

"Doris!" Principal Donahue bellows from his doorway, jerking us back into the present. "Get Dr. McCleery on the line—"

I reach for a black-foiled mint, hoping to steady my pounding heart. Why would Donahue need to speak to Uncle Mark anyway?

"—And send in The Delinquent."

Ah, yes. That's my other nickname.

Original, I know.

My heart continues to pound against my rib cage, but it has nothing to do with nerves about being called into the principal's office. No, this chest pain is something different. Something life-threatening. I can only hope that Mrs. Kelso's defibrillator certifications are up to date, because if I die on shag carpeting installed by the lowest bidder it would be a travesty. Fitting, but a travesty.

The mountains of reports teetering at the front corner of Donahue's desk beg me to knock into them. I find nothing more beautiful than sending reams of paper spiraling in a chaotic rhythm to the floor. Well, except for maybe watching the giant of a man pick it all up.

But not today.

Today, foreign encounters of the bizarre kind have thrown off my thirst for small acts of violence and disruption.

"Cigarettes, Gigi?" he says, followed by an exasperated sigh. "You don't even smoke."

I choose not to disagree with him. When I lie my throat burns like the hot coals I almost swallowed at the Fourth of July barbecue involving intoxication, a dare, and a poorly executed circus trick. The cameras in the school don't lie either. And the pack of cigarettes on his desk along with the zebra-print lighter carved with "Gigi" sitting on top of the green folder? Cold, hard evidence.

I shrug. "I like the smell."

His eyebrows melt into his protruding forehead. Small children have gone lost in there, never to return.

"You like the smell of cigarettes?"

And so, begins our daily staring contest. Each of us searching for the missing plate in the other's armor before loosing the final black iron arrow. These battles have gone on for hours. Sometimes days. Often weeks. Neither one of us willing to admit defeat. Neither one of us willing to yield.

That is until today.

The intercom squawks during a particularly intense clash. Donahue narrows his eyes, still glaring at me as he presses the button.

"Yes, Doris?"

"Dr. Donahue, Dr. McCleery is on the line."

The bulging vein in his forehead thrums into action. "Miss Brennan, you and I aren't through with this conversation. Tell Mrs. Kelso to add another ten days of after-school detention to your sentence."

"So, that puts me at five years past my graduation date?"

He ignores my smart retort, more interested in speaking with Uncle Mark instead.

"Hello, Dr. McCleery. Yes, I wanted to talk to you about Breas, your foreign exchange student?"

That's the hunky Irishman's name. Figures.

"He and I have had several differences in opinion. I would appreciate it if you could come in to discuss the matter further."

Stunned into silence, I sit as a delinquent-in-waiting.

Fire alarms have gone off. Food fights have broken out. Angry parents have banged on his door, and still, after one of us claims victory, he always, I mean *always*, begins with his "Make Good Choices" lecture and leads into "This is the last time, young lady. Next stop, Juvie."

But he skips the lecture and doesn't even dismiss me with his trademark off-you-go wave, because he's completely absorbed in his conversation with Uncle Mark.

And speaking of Uncle Mark, why did he fail to mention Breas's arrival last night at dinner or the half dozen other nights last week? Having some stranger live with you seems a pretty important event in one's life, but no. He said nothing. He acted as Principal Donahue is acting now. As if I am invisible. As if Breas's housing situation has nothing to do with me.

And as for that initial attraction I felt?

It vanished the moment he claimed me as his.

I, Gigi Brennan, belong to no one.

CHAPTER 2

Past Infractions

Lizzie pulls a binder out of her locker. "So, did you get in trouble?"

I flop back against the wall. "The day I get in any real trouble is the day I find Jesus."

"That soft spot for your mom still gets him hard, huh?"

I shove her across the hall. "Ewww!"

She rushes over and grabs my arm. "Oh my god, what if Donahue is your father?"

I jerk out of her grasp. "That's not even funny. My dad's some drug addict the birth vessel met at a crack house. Besides, Donahue's like seven feet tall and half walrus." I gesture to my five-foot-nothing frame.

She swooshes my cropped white hair up and flicks the short black hair underneath. "Maybe your mom had sex with a skunk."

I backpedal away from her. "You're a bitch, you know that?"

"That's what friends are for. We acknowledge our weaknesses and still love each other. Have you caught wind of the new guy yet?"

"Caught wind of him? Are we really continuing this skunk analogy?"

She winks at me. "Mrs. Bauguess impresses on us the importance of word choice. And, you didn't answer my question."

Just the mention of the "new guy" makes me feel woozy. "He told me I was 'his.'"

"What?" Her fingers dig into my arm as she catches me with her laser-beam stare. One of these days I really think she's going to slice me in half with it.

"He blew out of Donahue's office, took one blazing breath as he stalked across the office, and said, 'You're mine,' in his Irish accent before drifting out the door."

"What did you do?"

"For the first minute I sat like a dumb ass with my thumb up my bum. Then my brain started working again, and I regretted not kicking him in the Good and Plenties when I had the chance."

She snorts out of her nose. She has the best laughs. Even when I'm mad and want to break something, which is actually quite often, she makes me laugh every single time.

"Gi, he's gorgeous—*and* Irish. That alone makes him an object of interest. Did you see his broad shoulders? He's a delicious piece of man-flesh," she says, biting her wrist.

I slam my locker shut. "Exactly. Where's the damaged soul? Where are the layers of scar tissue?"

Her lips curl up. "You like the ones you can love and leave."

I place my hand over my heart. "True. Leaving is quite

satisfying. Imagine if your parents knew you were best friends with a girl whose flower has been plucked more times than a wedding bouquet."

She punches my arm. "Gi, don't joke about my parents' moral compass. If they knew I was friends with you, we both know what would happen."

Her Jehovah's Witness parents prohibit any and all interaction with non-JWs outside of school unless the JW is ministering a non-JW. I get a lot of ministering. Well, her parents don't know she's helping *the* Gigi Brennan. They think she's helping a troubled youth and not the daughter of the whore who evidently used to be their friend. But really, I am one and the same.

A wave of unease falls over me as a fresh breeze smelling of a late-day sun shower replaces the stale, moldy, sweat smell of the hallway. My heart thumps into a frantic double beat. Everything around me grows cloudy, sort of out-of-body, like I'm watching all this weird shit happen to me and I can't do anything about it.

As if that's not cause for a panic attack, I forget how to inhale. Seriously forget how to pull oxygen into my lungs and release carbon dioxide. All made worse by scorching fingertips trailing along the curve of my jaw.

"Mine," a hot, suffocating breath whispers in my ear. My eyes roll back in my head, and everything goes black.

CHAPTER 3

riends of Three

THE AMMONIA LEAVES me gasping for air.

"You'll feel better in a few minutes," Mrs. Paige says, patting my arm.

"What happened?" I ask her, but I don't recognize my voice. It sounds like I swallowed a mouthful of sand, and I haven't willingly done that since I was at least four.

Before she can answer, a pale-faced Scott bursts into the room, followed closely by Lizzie and Ryan. "What happened? Is she okay?"

"Gigi's fine, but she needs some breathing room."

Scott grabs my left hand, Lizzie grabs my right, and Ryan grips my blanket-covered feet.

Mrs. Paige rolls her eyes. "So much for space. To answer your question, Gigi, I don't know what happened. Usually a sudden drop in blood pressure causes someone to faint. I think you're fine—some rest, something to eat, and your grandmother wants you to drink this."

She hands me a steaming mug of tea.

"You called Gram?"

She nods. "Of course I did. When Rose Brennan's granddaughter faints, I'm going to call my friend. Will you let her know I need more tea?"

I glance at the handmade mug with the blue-green wash and Celtic knot stamp. It appears that Gram not only supplies Mrs. Paige with her cure-all tea, but her pottery as well. But Mrs. Paige's version of the tea makes me wince. Lavender and lemon verbena mask the scent of the more noxious herbs, but not the bitterness.

"Did she send you any of her honey?"

She removes the arm pressure cuff. "No, dear, just the tea."

I sip some more, and the rough edges of the nightmare fall away.

Thank god, because that creepy otherworldly crap was too much for me. For as long as I can remember, I've drunk Gram's tea three times a day without fail. Well, mostly without fail. This morning, after I sat my mug on the windowsill to water a plant, Boo Bear knocked it over in his blind attempt—no really, he's blind—to get a scratch. I mopped up the mess but didn't bother to brew another cup.

Scott plops down on the bed next to me. "Dad's on his way. He'll drop you off to Gram. I'd go home with you, but I have practice after school."

Ryan ruffles Scott's shaggy auburn hair. "And damn if he doesn't need it. He couldn't throw for shit last Friday."

Lizzie cracks her gum. She chews it like a fiend during the school day to make up for missed opportunities after school, because according to her parents' JW philosophy, gum chewing leads to sin.

"Boys, Gi doesn't want to hear about football or your inability to make a touchdown."

Ryan wraps his arm around her and pulls her close. "Sweetheart, we don't make touchdowns. Scott throws it, I catch it, and ... magic."

She lets him nestle her into his chest before winking at me as she swats his arm.

This flirting has been going on for months. All the while Ryan's made his way through most of the school's female population with notions of parental rebellion, because he represents everything the majority of the townspeople are not, and Lizzie's gone out with half the marching band and three-quarters of the stoners, chess club, and motocross bikers with notions of, well, boy-craziness. Her JW parents might prohibit her interaction with non-JWs after school and on weekends, but during the school day and after lights out, she manages to find the time.

I cradle Gram's mug between my hands. This little piece of her grounds me to this tiny, sterile room with my three best friends surrounding me.

"I hate that Uncle Mark has to cancel class to come get me."

Scott shrugs. "Dad was on his way anyway. Evidently someone named Breas, who will be living with us, got under Donahue's skin more than you, and that's saying something."

Breas's words come flooding back to me with a pull of familiarity. I take another sip of tea, and the impressions fall away.

I know in the United States possession is nine-tenths of the law. I wonder if Ireland follows the same laws we do.

CHAPTER 4

*J*udgment and Bitch Moves

UNCLE MARK PULLS into our driveway. "Are you sure you don't want me to walk you inside?"

"If I can't make it into the house stone sober, I'll be in deep shit this weekend."

"Gigi, I don't like you talking like that."

I tug at the car door handle and hop out. "Well, lucky for me, you're just my next-door neighbor and not my dad."

His hands grip the steering wheel. I peek back inside, which at my height doesn't require much ducking.

"I'm sorry, Uncle Mark. Sometimes I'm just a bitch. Thanks for the ride home."

He forces a smile, but hurt still lurks in his eyes. Nothing like feeling even more like an asshole before snack time.

"You're welcome, Gigi. Anytime."

I slam the door and stroll up the path.

"You know that, right?" he shouts.

I turn back to see him standing outside his car, ready to run over and catch me if I fall. It reminds me of when he taught me to ride a bike without training wheels. He'd run up and down the street with me all day no matter how fast I peddled or how much I whined for him to let me go. He refused to leave my side until I could ride without wobbling. Even weeks later, he stayed within grabbing range.

"I'll be here for you no matter what."

I give him my trademark impish smirk. "I know, Uncle Mark. I know you will be."

His lips rise into another smile, but he seems sad too. "I'll see you at dinner. Meatless Monday?"

His comment makes me laugh. It's always Meatless Monday at our house, even when it's not Monday. "Gram's been experimenting with quinoa and tofu."

He winces. "Maybe we'll pass on dinner."

"That might be the safest option." I don't add that I'd rather they skipped eating at our house the entire length of Breas's stay—I've already hurt his feeling enough for one day.

Laughing, he climbs back into his car. "Take care, Gigi."

I nod and watch him reverse down the driveway, drive thirty feet down the street, and pull in next door. He waves from his stone path as if he didn't just leave me. Smiling to myself, I wave back.

Scott and Uncle Mark moved in sometime before I was born. We're not related or anything. I just call him "Uncle Mark" and Scott calls Gram "Gram" because we spend so much time together. They eat most meals at our house, including holidays and birthdays. Scott even has his own room here. Uncle Mark's a professor of Celtic Mythology and Folklore at the University of Pittsburgh, so he travels to far-off places to study old books and ancient artifacts and to present his findings to people interested in academic stuff, or as I like to call them, Irish Geeks. In fact, he goes to Ireland three or four times a year. He still hasn't taken me with him, even though I've begged him at least a million times. He says Gram would miss me too much, which I suppose is true. Plus, she doesn't leave the property, so she relies on family and friends to go shopping for her. She'd be lost without me.

My only consolation is that he doesn't take Scott with him either.

Not quite ready to go inside, I stop to deadhead the geranium still in bloom on the porch railing. Mid-pluck, my eyes drift over to the front yard of our other neighbor's house. The tiny patch of grass, once my birthing place, is now hidden behind a tall white picket fence. It still must infuriate the church freak that a wild hippie girl fell to the snowy frozen ground that first day of February sixteen years ago. The birth of the fatherless heathen, the final insult.

A barely formed shadow hides behind the thin, white curtains. She's always watching. Always judging.

My sweatshirt slips down my arm exposing one of my tattoos. Not that she needs additional ammunition to hate the fatherless heathen. The tattoo just confirms what she already knows.

My shoulders round in on themselves. I feel myself breaking down, which frustrates me even more than my judgmental neighbor. I don't know why I let the demons snap at my exposed throat.

Actually, that's a lie. I know why. It's freaking exhausting always being The Delinquent. To pretend I don't hear the ugly nicknames and the mean laughter. To pretend I don't see the pointing fingers or notice the scratches on the bathroom wall with the creative tag, "For a good time call Skunk Girl 555-555-5555."

The impenetrable fortress I constructed, lie by lie, occasionally fissures along the carefully knit seams. My breath starts to catch in short impatient gasps. Some unknown force takes a strangle hold on my throat. Carbon dioxide leaves my body, but no oxygen replaces it.

I blink back tears.

Not today.

Not now.

A panic attack would be the shitty topper to an even shittier day. I try to breathe through my nose, taking wisps of breath in. Wisps of breath out. I grip the purple railing with the rainbow-colored spindles, digging so tightly into it I'd get a splinter if it wasn't freshly painted. It grounds me to this world.

This is me.

This is who I am.

I take one full breath in. One full breath out. Then another. And another. The strangle hold begins to release, and oxygen slowly seeps back into my lungs.

I'd never admit it to my old therapist, but her little breathing tricks work. When I'm finished almost suffocating to death, I decide to get inside before my brain and heart enter another epic battle of their own again.

"Move, Sphinx," I tell the fat cat who took up residence on the front doormat. She stretches across the threshold instead. She likes to pretend she can't hear. She hears just fine. It's two blind eyes that make it hard for her to see.

And yes, I have a blind cat and a blind dog. I also own a hamster with a walker in addition to a menagerie of other homeless and handicapped pets that have adopted Gram and me as their caretakers. You got a problem with that?

Good. I didn't think so.

I step over Sphinx. She mews a complaint before quickly returning to her dreams of world domination.

"Gram," I shout from the front door. "Hey, Gram!"

When her singsong, "Hello" doesn't reach me, I drop my

bag and keep walking through the house to the kitchen. The comfort of home pushes the final edges of the panic attack away.

Boo Bear wobbles over to me, his tail wagging in greeting. I pick him up, grab the steaming mug of tea Gram left for me on the counter, and follow the path to the herb garden.

"Hello, dear," Gram sings before I even round the corner. "Feeling better?"

I drop Boo Bear in her lap and fold myself onto the ground in front of her. The sweet smell of lavender fills the space between us.

"Yeah, I guess. Did you know Uncle Mark was getting a foreign exchange student?"

She pushes a few flyaways back into her ponytail. "He called me this morning. Breas is the son of one of Mark's childhood friends. He showed up just after you and Scott left for school. He insisted Mark enroll him today." She stops and smiles at me. "I think your uncle spun tales of adventures to a young Breas, and now that he's grown, he wants to experience this Great America on his own."

"I don't like him."

She scratches Boo Bear behind the ears. He pushes his head into her hand and purrs. The dog is part cat, I tell you.

"You will."

"I'm not so sure."

"You'll get to know him tonight at dinner."

"Gram," I say, trying not to whine, "do we have to?"

She carefully places Boo Bear on the path and stands up. He nudges his nose into the back of her leg—his signal it's time to get moving.

"Why don't you go into the greenhouse and cut some roses for the vase. The other ones seek to return to Earth."

"Are you trying to distract me?"

She winks at me. "My dear, I have no idea what you're talking about. Drink your tea and get me some flowers please."

I take another sip, feeling more and more like myself. I know it's a combination of herbs Gram's blended together. The chamomile, lemon verbena, and lavender all have soothing qualities. I don't know what the other herbs do, but combined together, the blend makes me feel better. More like me.

Although most of the time I don't know who that is.

CHAPTER 5

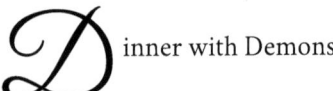 inner with Demons

A PILE of yellow roses lies strewn across the old worktable. I add heather and a few sprigs of fern, then decide aster would provide some good contrast.

"So, this is where you hide," a male voice says with an Irish accent much thicker than Uncle Mark's.

For point twenty-seven seconds my heart flutters in my chest. Then I find my anger with a capital V for Vengeance.

I jab more roses into the arrangement. "This is a gross invasion of my privacy."

He steps up alongside me. "Is it?"

I grab another rose stalk and squeeze. The thorns bite into my palm. "Damn it." I suck the fresh cuts. The taste of rust fills my mouth. "What are you doing here?"

"Fetching you for dinner."

I shove the rest of the flowers into the vase. "Ironically, I've lost my appetite."

He moves closer. "Shall we make use of this table in some other manner then?"

"That's it—" I stomp on his foot.

He doesn't wince. He doesn't scowl. He especially doesn't yelp.

He *does* wear a cocky grin I'd like to knock off.

"Steel-toed," he murmurs.

I growl. Actually growl. Then I remember my words. "You better back the fuck up."

"Everything all right in here?" Scott asks from the doorway. He glances from me with my scissors to Breas with his cocky grin and back to me.

"Everything's fine, laddie," Breas says.

I point my scissors at the Irishman, then him. "Did you know about this?"

Scott backs away, knowing what I'm capable of when armed with sharp objects. "No, no. I had nothing to do with it. I didn't know anything about him until Mrs. Kelso called me down to the nurse's office when you fainted. I already told you that."

Betrayal rushes through me. I set the scissors down before I do anything I might regret. "Why didn't your dad tell us?"

He lifts his shoulders. "I don't know."

"I can answer that question," Breas says, inserting himself into the conversation. "He didn't know until I showed up at his door this morning."

Scott folds his arms and leans against the door frame, sliding into his casual, conversational act. He eases his victims into giving him everything he wants to know. He's not a patented ass-kicker like myself, though his method often gets him better results—I really can't stand that about him.

"How do you know my dad?"

Breas smiles. "He and I have known each other for a long time. A very long time."

I pick at my nails to draw attention to their very sharp dagger points. I may not be holding the scissors anymore, but I am still capable of maiming. "Funny that it's the first time we've ever heard of you."

"We've met before." He glances back and forth between us. "We've *all* met before."

Scott and I share a long look.

Scott doesn't remember him anymore than I do. However, he's far too polite to mention this fact to Breas.

Luckily, I'm not.

"It's amazing how easily you were forgotten. Remember that." I pick up the vase and start walking toward the door, but the stupid idiot blocks my path.

"Move," I growl.

He shoves his hands in his pockets.

I brush past him.

Well, "brush" isn't the best word. I elbow him in the gut.

He drops low to my ear. "Is that any way to welcome a guest?"

"You're no guest of mine," I hiss through clenched teeth, his little claiming scene from this morning still fresh in my mind. "I don't like you."

"You will," he laughs. "You don't have a choice."

"I've got a choice all right, and mine includes a shallow grave in the backyard."

He winks at me. "You are a naughty one. Exactly how I like them."

If the vase wasn't Gram's favorite, I'd smash it over his head and wouldn't feel an ounce of guilt about it.

He claps Scott on the back. "She's something."

"I wouldn't if I were you," Scott warns him. He knows how quickly things can turn.

They follow me down the path. Scott peppers him with questions about Ireland and how he knows his dad again—Breas still didn't answer that one. By the time we get into the house, Gram's already set the table. In addition to the tofu and quinoa, she made some other dishes involving potatoes, onions, and carrots—I suppose in honor of our "special" guest, though he certainly doesn't deserve it. After placing the vase in the center of the table, I glare at her to make her realize exactly the punishment I've suffered as a result of Breas.

She tilts her head away from me instead and slips into her chair. "Why doesn't everyone take a seat?"

Mark and Scott sit in their usual spots, leaving only two seats next to each other. I sigh, unable to believe the mistreatment I'm forced to suffer through even at dinnertime.

Round tables work for family and friends who enjoy exchanging pleasantries about the day in a cyclical, round-about way—there's nothing pleasant about sitting next to some asshole who keeps invading your space and insinuating you're together and who also, for some reason that you can't possibly fathom, you're inexplicably drawn to, which makes you detest his presence even more. I wish we had a rectangular table with sharp corners to separate me from Irish ding-dongs.

Breas makes himself comfortable by sitting as close to me as he can without sitting on my lap—which he probably considered but didn't want to draw too much attention to himself. It's only the gentle touch of Gram's palm against the top of my hand that keeps me from stabbing him.

After she thanks the day for the blessings of our plentiful table—although I strongly disagree with her—we fill our plates and eat in silence. I attribute the lack of conversation to Mr. Rat Bastard's presence. It's obvious Uncle Mark, Scott, and Gram don't know what to say to him any more than I do. With any luck, they'll come to their senses and kick him out before he can cause any more havoc.

Our "guest," and I use that term loosely, eats and drinks like it's normal not to talk during a meal. He makes himself right at home, taking seconds of quinoa, before adding some to my plate without even asking.

"There you go, Gigi," he says.

I stop the heaping spoon in midair. "No, thank you," I yell, but it's too late. Quinoa, celery, carrots, and currants splatter across the table. All because of the stupid oaf. "Are you happy now?"

"Gigi, you aren't being particularly friendly to our guest," Gram says.

He flashes me a reckless grin.

I glare at him. "I'm not feeling particularly hungry either. Excuse me."

Before Gram can guilt me into staying, I disappear from the table. She might not be the punishing type, but her disappointment carries a burden far greater than any grounding or reprimand. I hate disappointing her. The birth vessel did that enough to last a lifetime.

When I'm in a bad mood, I go to the greenhouse, but Breas's presence corrupted it. Tomorrow I'll need to purify the space with incense and candles. Until then it's off-limits, unless of course I want to torture myself some more, but I believe I've experienced enough pain and suffering for one day. The jackass has never been in my bedroom, but one floor of separation is not enough distance between us. The attic puts me two stories away from the table and the Irish asshole. And if he should find me, I'll fling one of Gram's silver daggers at him.

Actually, that's not a bad plan. No court would try me if I claim self-defense.

When I plop down into the worn velvet chair by the window, dust motes dance in the early evening light. I try to catch them with my fingers in the hopes that tiny sparkling fairies will grant me my wish of ridding the house of unwanted guests. After several minutes of catching and releasing potential fairies, a rumble of laughter echoes from downstairs, and I know my wish hasn't been granted. Big surprise. There are wish givers and there are wish receivers, and then there is the lint between the wishes. Can you guess what I am?

From my perch, the corner window overlooks the greenhouse and the gardens. The coneflower and ligularia are still in bloom. It looks like the bee balm, rudbeckia, and cilantro are ready for seed collection. This weekend before Gram and I prep the ground for next spring's crops, I'll need to clean the layer of pollen off the greenhouse roof. I'd ask Scott to help, but the Steelers play at one o'clock on Sunday. Without fail, I'll be elbow deep in compost, while he's elbow deep in a bucket of wings along with Ryan, Uncle Mark, and with any luck, Breas.

Maybe Scott can persuade his coach to add Breas to his team's roster. That way there's no chance of him showing up at the greenhouse or the garden uninvited, and believe me, he won't be invited.

I can just avoid him at mealtimes. Eating's overrated anyway.

Just thinking about him makes me want to break something.

Stupid boy.

I kick the trunk—find very little satisfaction—so I kick the support post.

Still not enough.

I slam my fist into the post. Pain spreads through my fingers and down my hands. Pain is good. Pain means I'm alive. Breaking my hand means I can't take the math test tomorrow, which isn't a big deal. But I also wouldn't be able to garden with Gram this weekend, which is a big deal, especially since she says the moon will be at the prime phase for fall planting.

Ugh. I really can't stand that bastard. He makes me so mad. I could just…

I stomp down.

Clunk.

That was fun.

I stomp again. A floorboard flies up and almost smashes me in the face.

I get it. Stupid karma.

I kick the loose floorboard to the side. It ricochets off the old steamer trunk and whacks my shin.

Yep, I never learn.

As I bend over to nurse my knee, I notice a book shoved between the floorboards. Curious, because as I've already told you, I never learn, my fingers grow tingly as I stretch to reach it. A strange, magnetic energy seeps up my fingers into my hands and up my arms. The instant I make contact, an electric charge knocks me backward.

What the hell?

Shaking my head like Boo Bear after he smacks his into the pet door, I'm temporarily stunned, but no real impression is made. I wipe off the dust from the bottom of my Docs to ground me to the floor. In my mind, this makes good, practical sense. I pinch my lips together, because in case you didn't know, pinched lips help ward off creepy paranormal shit. With intense concentration, I grab the book. Energy rushes through me. Before it knocks me over, I collapse back into the chair with it safely in hand.

And I said I couldn't learn. Shows you what I know.

CHAPTER 6

ractured Stroll Down Memory Lane

THE DOOR at the base of the stairs squeaks open.

"Everything all right up there?" Uncle Mark calls up to me.

It might be my imagination, but the book vibrates at the sound of his voice.

"Everything's fine. Just needed some time to myself."

The stairs creak on his way up. I shove the book into the cushion because I'm not sure if I should be reading it or not, and I'd rather figure that out on my own than be parented by my next-door neighbor again.

He stops at the top of the landing and smiles at me. "You sure you're okay?"

I nod more enthusiastically than the situation warrants. Certainly, more enthusiastically than I've ever responded to any question. "Yep, one hundred percent. I skipped breakfast this morning."

He raises his eyebrows. "Gram tells me you missed your tea too."

I drop my eyes, realize how guilty I look, and quickly lift my chin. "Boo Bear knocked it over. I never refilled it."

His forehead bunches. He has the easiest tells. He'd never win at poker.

"Make sure you eat your breakfast and always drink your tea. You need to keep your strength up."

"Yes, Uncle Mark," I say in the same singsong tone as Gram's.

He shakes his head, knowing exactly who I'm pretending to be.

"Take care, Gi. I'll see you in the morning," he says, turning to leave.

Suddenly, I don't want him to go. Not before I apologize. "Hey, Uncle Mark?"

He turns around. "Yes?"

"I'm sorry for what I said earlier. You're a lot more than 'just my next-door neighbor.'"

His eyes tear up. He's a sensitive one, isn't he? That's where Scott gets it from. Not necessarily a bad thing, just an emotion that freaky orphans like me can't possess.

"That means a lot, Gigi," he says. "I …" He tries again. "I …" He swallows whatever sentiment he's about to say and starts anew. "I'll see you in the morning."

"Sounds good. Bye!" I wave using all the telepathic telekinetic teleforce ability I can muster to get him down the stairs and out the door.

He smiles once more before leaving.

I fall back into the chair, stunned. He bought one of the most bogus performances of my lifetime. Maybe that tele-whatever-you-want-to-call-it really works. Then again, maybe he just wanted to go home and couldn't wait for the first opportunity to leave. Seems to be my theme song.

As soon as the attic door closes, I yank out the book and flop it open across my lap. The sucker presses against my thighs like a lazy, overfed beast. It's older than any book I've ever held. To most people that may not sound very impressive, but for me, it's significant. Uncle Mark studies ancient texts for a living. He travels all over the world just to study them. He and Gram also own extensive collections of ancient books, fairy tales, and dictionaries, which is probably why people give them theirs for safekeeping.

Scott and I learned at a young age how to handle and care for old books along with a basic knowledge of how to "date" a manuscript. I rub my hand along my jeans to remove any food residue or other oils before handling the paper. Then I carefully lift a sheet between my fingers. The paper's too thick to be woven fiber. I trail my nail along the length of it. It doesn't catch on any patterns or dimples, so the book predates laid paper, which started being used around the 1550s. Could be skin. I read somewhere that scholars and priests sometimes used human skin. Horrific, yet fascinating.

I close the cover and let my palms hover over it. The strange tingling returns, but it's not the overwhelming electric shock I felt when I first found it. It's more like static. Static I can handle.

With my fingertips, I trace the letter impressions with remnants of gold flecks ground deep into the pores of the leather. Whatever the title was is now lost. Something in another language. I recognize the symbol though. That I know well. As well as the tattoo on my left shoulder.

I finger my Celtic triskele tattoo. Not because I can feel the impression on my skin, but because I need confirmation that it's still there. Lizzie didn't want me to get it. She was afraid we'd get caught. Sneaking out of her parents' home while they slept peacefully with the naïve belief that their little Lizzie was safe and sound in bed was one thing. Never knowing that she lifted their car keys before she even climbed the stairs was another. The realization that their sweet, innocent Lizzie was at a rave in South Side with her best friend, the daughter of a whore, would cause dual cardiac arrests and warrant an exorcism.

But honestly, it wasn't my fault I got the tattoo. It was Ink or Die's fault. I mean, I was an impressionable teen who left a rave to grab some fries and pop from The O when we passed by the twenty-four-hour tattoo parlor. Lizzie begged me not to go in, but I didn't have a choice. If I didn't get inked, I'd die. Why risk it? And that triskele called to me. The guidance counselors always advised us to listen to our inner voice. I did what I was told.

Besides, the symbol on the cover confirms what I already suspected: I was supposed to get the tattoo.

I should probably get one on my right shoulder. I'd hate to upset the natural rhythms of the universe. And after I show Lizzie this book, she'll probably want to get one too. After all, ink or die.

On the inside cover, someone drew a different Celtic knot. I don't know the period. I'm not a master like Uncle Mark, but it reminds me of one of the symbols in Gram's old recipe book that she used to keep in her nightstand. The one I found back when I still romanticized about my mom's disappearance. (Read: naïve and stupid.) I figured that if I could learn more about her, I might be able to find her and ask her to come back or to take me with her. (Again, read: naïve and stupid.)

Gram's room was the obvious place to look. I spent hours in there searching for something—anything—that could give me some hint or clue where my mom was or even what she looked like. I piled boxes on top of one another and climbed to the top shelves of her closet. I banged on walls for secret hiding places. I dug through her dresser drawers.

I didn't go up to the attic. Had I known that the most terrifying monsters lurked in the hallways of school and not on our top floor, I could have found this book years ago, but that's a half dozen therapy sessions I'll never work out.

When my search came up empty, I grew frantic. I tore at her sheets. I ripped pillows off her bed. I knocked over a lamp, sending hundreds of shards of shattered light bulb across the floor. Then I panicked. Getting caught terrified me. Disappointing Gram was akin to point-blank execution. I hid the evidence of my tantrum as best as I could. Sweeping broken glass under the rug. Shoving feathers beneath the bed. When I set the lamp with its bent shade back, a calmness washed over me. Like I already knew the answer. Like if only I listened to my heart I'd find what I was searching for. That's when I found the old recipe book with the picture of my mom tucked in between the pages in the drawer of her nightstand.

Gram never once mentioned the broken light bulb or the trashed room. In the months that followed, I returned to the photo of my mom hundreds of times, memorizing every line on her face. Each strand of her hair. I searched for hidden messages or some hint as to why she wasn't with me. I cradled her picture in my hands, like a favorite baby doll as I flipped through the pages of that old recipe book. I prayed that the answer to her disappearance was tucked somewhere within the pages. I discovered the answer three months later when Kensey called my mom a crack whore. A crack whore who'd abandoned her daughter.

As far as I know, the ripped pieces of that photograph are the only evidence that the crack whore ever existed.

Well, with the exception of one barely surviving thing.

My breath catches. Oxygen stops coming in. I try to breath. Still can't. I try again. The roots of a panic attack want to sprout, but I won't let it win. Not this time. I take a deep breath and remind myself that the crack whore doesn't rule here anymore.

I do.

I am the master of my own story.

I turn to the next page. A dedication. A warning. I can't tell. My fingers hover above the handwritten message. It feels more cautionary than welcoming. Of course I flip to the next page. You already know full well I never learn.

Page after page the images and the text come to life. Numbers I recognize. Symbols trigger impressions as if I know what the authors are trying to impart to the reader. Dozens of handwritten notes are scrawled in the margins. Equations and words, sometimes entire passages, are crossed out and corrected. Images of animals, Celtic knots, crosses, and people cover every page. There are long lists with ingredients for recipes. But more than recipes.

"Spells," a voice inside my head murmurs.

"Spells," I whisper back.

CHAPTER 7

dventures by Candlelight

SPELL AFTER SPELL, the meanings become easy to understand, as if I knew the words long before ever finding the book. As if I've known this language all along. Like maybe I know this language better than my own. Like maybe it is my own.

There is light and darkness on every page. I see them in the pictures. I sense them in the words.

Something cannot be given without something else taken away. That much is clear. Each step of every spell comes with a rhythm. If the rhythm is broken there is great risk involved. The greater the power, the greater the risk.

The evening fades into night without me even being aware of its passing. When it's finally too dark to read, I arrange Gram's candles in a circle around me, lighting the yellow one first, followed by the red, then the blue. The green candle's crooked, so I reposition it before lighting it.

I'm methodical in my process because it feels important. It feels right.

The candles cast a warm glow around the room. I imagine the spell workers working by the same candlelight, dipping the tips of their pens into the ink, recording the steps of the spell in the precise order and with the exact ingredients down to the very last pinch of mugwort.

They must have slaved for hours over each spell.

How many times did they have to cast it until they got it right?

And from the markings in the margins, they didn't always get it right.

How long did it take them to create the artwork on the pages?

Like the two-page spread of a man and a woman entwined together on a bed of pillows with two female servants standing behind them. One holds a grapevine with lush, fertile fruit attached to it; the other, a tray with wine goblets and a pitcher. The man nuzzles the woman's neck while his hands explore her body, but the woman holds her body stiff, her gaze far off in the distance. As if she's reluctant to his advances.

I recognize the emotion in her face. It is the way I feel every day of my life.

She's resigned herself to defeat.

CHAPTER 8

*D*aydreams and Nightmares

I KNEW *he'd be here. He can't resist the beauty of the sisters even when they are not the prize he seeks.*

His relentless pursuit grows tiresome. His charms, his flirtations, do not fill me with romantic notions of true affection. It is more that he is the hunter and I am the hunted, and sometimes even prey chooses to get caught.

I drop down beside him on the bed soft as clouds. He plucks a grape off the vine and offers it to me. It is a game he's played many times before, but never with favorable results. At least not from me. Rather than rebuff his advance, I wrap my lips around the fruit. His gray eyes mirror the lustful thoughts of my own mind.

We press our bodies against each other, moving in a slow, seductive rhythm. It is as it should be. At least as the stars have aligned it. At least as I have allowed it.

"Breas," I breathe into his ear.

"I knew you'd come," he whispers, his hot breath heating me to the depths of my core. *"You will always come."*

"Coming?" Scott shouts from the front door.

My eyes spring open as Sphinx claws my lap. It's the third time this morning I've slipped back into my dream from last night, and I've only been up for ten minutes.

Gram places the back of her hand on my forehead. "Are you okay, Gigi? Do you have a fever?"

I drink more tea to fortify my nerves. "I'm fine. I didn't sleep well last night."

At all actually. I stayed up most of the night reading. When I finally slipped off into sleep, the dream—well, nightmare starring Breas and yours truly—made me restless. Only copious amounts of caffeine will get me through the day. The dregs from the bottom of the Quikmart carafe are the only cure for this lack-of-sleep-over.

Hangovers too.

"Could I have a travel mug for school?"

She hands me my favorite purple mug with the words "F — You" etched on it. "Already made you one. Finish that cup and take this one with you. If you don't feel well, go to Mrs. Paige and have another."

"Thanks, Gram."

Scott walks into the kitchen. "Coming anytime today?" He leans over to give Gram a kiss.

She pats his cheek. "Good morning, dear. Want a muffin?"

He grabs three off the plate. "I'll never turn down one of your baked goods."

I shove my arms into my backpack. "You never turn down food period."

"Oh, you two," she laughs. "Get going to school."

"I'm trying to get there, Gram. Your granddaughter's slowing me down."

I smack his arm. He jumps away, knowing all too well that I drag my nails across skin for full impact—and the most pain—but he's not fast enough. My hand just nicks him, and he has the fresh trails of blood to prove it.

His eyes go wide as he rubs his arm. "Gi, you got me."

"You know not to mess with me in the morning. Anytime in fact." I bend down to kiss Gram. "Bye. Love you."

"Love you, Gigi. Love you, Scott."

Tucking my thumbs under my backpack straps, I wiggle my fingers at him in warning. "Let's go, squirrel boy. You can forage for muffins later."

He swallows his mouthful and follows me to his truck. I climb in, but he doesn't close the door behind me. Not that I'm a damsel in distress that needs saving, because I am most definitely not. It's just that Scott likes to take care of people. It makes him happy, and who am I to deny him. Plus, I'm lazy, so there's that.

But does Scott close the door? Noooo, he just walks over to the driver's side as if there isn't a major problem with the situation.

I point to the door. "What's the big deal?"

"Well..." he says, "ummm..."

While he stutters an excuse, Breas slips in beside me, smelling of rain on a hot summer day. An image of the two of us tangled in each other's arms flashes through my mind. My cheeks flush, but it's the explosion of sensation that rushes through me the moment he touches my arm that's the problem. I should have known Breas would go to school with Scott, and by default, me. Comatose-brain me didn't realize it until I was smashed between the two of them in Scott's pickup.

"Gi, you look like shit, by the way," Scott says.

"Not all of us wake up pretty."

"Clearly," Breas adds.

I grind my jaw and pretend I didn't hear him.

No, I do better than that. I pretend he doesn't exist.

The woozy feeling in my stomach is the result of too much tea this morning. I do not possess anything remotely resembling feelings or attraction. I hate him, remember?

"Gi, would you show me around school this morning? I've forgotten where my classes are," Breas says in his stupid Irish accent.

Scott catches my eye in the rearview mirror. He shakes his head just enough for me to notice, but it's a waste of effort. Certain things I will not let go. Ever.

A chosen handful call me "Gi." Breas is not one of them.

He waves his hand in front of my face. "Alloo? Can you hear me?"

"Careful," Scott says, "she's not a morning person, and FYI, she does bite."

"I look forward to it," Breas murmurs in my ear.

Another flash of our lips mashed against each other pops into my head. A burn inches up my neck. It takes everything in my power not to lunge at him and either kiss him or burrow my nails into his larynx.

"Don't go there, man," Scott says. "It won't go well for you.

"Guess, I'll ask one of the lovely ladies I met last night. Any one of them would enjoy the opportunity to experience all I have to show them."

Sometimes I can't keep my mouth shut. "You were at my house last night, and I believe we've established that I will not be showing you anything except the backside of a door."

"Gi, you truly are protected, aren't you?"

Before I can react or respond or figure out what he means by "protected," he continues.

"After you abandoned us during dinner, I excused myself to attend a get-together I was invited to by some enthusiastic and very friendly classmates."

I bite my lip. I will not ask him. I will not ask him. I do not care. I do not. Then I find a loophole.

"Scott, did you go?"

"No, I had a paper due. Kensey invited him."

My stomach drops. "Kensey? You went to Kensey's house?"

He rubs my arm. I'm not going to lie. I wet my lips. It's like I lose my mind when he touches me.

"She does care. Don't worry, I have plenty left for you."

That is exactly what I'm afraid of. I want to hate him. I want to be repulsed by his flirtations. I want to fling my arms around him and find out if Irish kissing is better than French.

CHAPTER 9

 offee for Mickey

When we get out of the truck, Breas wraps his tentacles around me. The moment his skin touches mine, a warm fuzziness travels through me. I hate that my body betrays me when he's in close proximity.

Curse him and his Irishness.

I elbow him in the stomach and stomp away. His laugh circles around and follows me into the building. Scott murmurs a warning to him, but the damage has already been done. My inner voice has decided I will not remain in school today. And as we've already established, I always listen to my inner voice.

Lizzie's crouched down in front of her locker. When I get close, I wrap my fingers around her sleeve and pull. "Come on."

She fumbles to close the door before I drag her down the hall. "Where we going?"

"Somewhere."

"What about school?"

"What about it?"

"We have classes."

"So."

She tries to stop my rhythm, but her resistance reminds me of a ladybug just before someone flicks it with her finger.

"Come on." I tug her outside.

Fresh air rushes to greet us, making me feel like I am capable of achieving anything. Lizzie sucks in a breath of the cool morning air and sighs. She feels it too. Without me asking, she follows me to Scott's truck.

"Get in," I say.

"Does he know you're taking it?"

"Not really."

"Do you have the key?"

"I don't need it." I dig under the dashboard and disconnect the starter. I pull the wires out of my earring loops and squeeze them into the power connector.

"You've done this before," she says. It's not a question.

I shrug. "Once or twice."

I unfasten one of my necklaces, which is really a wire with two clips at the end. I'm more about utility than fashion. I connect one clip to one wire and bring down the second clip to the other one. The truck rumbles to life.

"That's a good boy," I murmur, patting the dashboard.

"Won't he realize his truck is missing?"

I pull out of the parking lot. "He has practice after school. We'll be back by the time he needs it."

"Where are we going?"

"Well, it's your first time skipping. Where do you want to go?"

"I don't even know where to begin."

"We start with coffee at the pond. There's something I want to show you."

I swear the spell book vibrates at the sound of my voice, just like it did with Uncle Mark.

AN HOUR LATER, we're sunbathing on the hood of the truck.

"So why did you force me out of school?"

"I didn't force you."

"You dug your nails into my arm and dragged me outside the building."

My fingers flutter across the truck hood. "I just didn't feel like going to school today."

She grabs my fingers. "You've never forced me to skip before."

I jerk my hand away from her and fumble with the zipper on my hoodie. "I thought you needed corrupting. You've been far too good lately."

"Gi, what's wrong?"

The tone of her voice. The care. The knowing. It's what finally wears me down.

"Breas came over for dinner last night."

She swallows her gasp. "How'd that go?"

"I walked out halfway through."

"What did he do?"

"He ... he ... the way he says stuff just makes me mad."

"I've always suspected you held some deep-seated hate against a particular ethnic group. Now I know. You're racist against the Irish," she says with a smile to her voice.

"Yes, I hate myself, my gram, Uncle Mark, and Scott. Definitely Scott."

"What is it about Breas that bothers you?"

"He's just so smug. Like a know-it-all. Like he knows me.

He makes me so mad." I clench my fist and think about smashing the hood. But then Scott would know I borrowed his truck, and he'd probably ask if I've "borrowed" it before, and I'd rather not lie to him. That whole burning throat thing is a real drag. Plus, he's rather fond of his old truck.

"Kensey and her clan are huge fans of him," she says.

"And that. Did you know he went to her house last night?"

"I thought he was at your house."

"After mine he went over. I can only imagine what she did with him." An image of the two of us entwined together pops into my head.

"If you hate him so much, why does it bother you?"

I narrow my eyes at her.

"Right, right. Forget I said anything."

I cover my face as I put my head against my knees. "When is this caffeine going to kick in?"

"Alloo, love! Fear not, for I come bearing gifts."

My heart stops as I look over at the Irishman carrying a cardboard tray with three steaming paper cups.

My spine immediately stiffens. "How'd you find us?"

"I saw you kidnap this one and steal Scott's truck."

"First, her name is Lizzie. Second, I didn't kidnap her. She came willingly."

Lizzie widens her eyes.

"Well, mostly willingly. And third, I didn't steal his truck. I borrowed it."

He raises an eyebrow. A very sexy eyebrow. "Does he know you borrowed it?"

I refuse to even dignify his question with an answer. Unfortunately, he takes my silence as an invitation to join us. As he pushes himself up next to me, his hand brushes mine before I snatch it away. A flash of our union last night triggers some unwanted physical responses.

"Stalk much?"

He laughs. "Your patterns have always been predictable."

My eyes slide over to Lizzie. I don't even know how to respond to that. I do know where Scott keeps the tire iron. That's something.

"Oh, how rude of me," he says. "Lizzie, I hope you like your coffee the same way Gi does."

Again, my eyes slide over to her. She, however, eagerly reaches for the cup with a greedy look in her eyes. Traitor.

When her eyes roll back in her head in pleasure, I snatch mine and chug. Hazelnut, espresso, cream, and just enough sugar to take the edge off the bitterness.

"Thank you," she murmurs in coffee bliss. Lizzie's parents don't allow coffee either. The heathens.

He leans back against the windshield. "My pleasure. I always take care of my ladies."

"Humpf," I blurt out before I remember that I'm not supposed to care what he says or what he thinks aside from the fact that I'm supposed to be ignoring him.

"I always do," he says in low voice full of meaning. He touches the exposed skin on my lower back.

I pretend not to notice, gulp down half my drink, then take off the lid and pour the rest of it over his mickey. Yes, I know the Irish word for penis.

"Argh," he yells. Even his curses sound Irish.

I shove off the truck and stomp away.

When I realize I'm alone, I turn around. "Coming, Lizzie?"

She grips her coffee in both hands as Breas bends over, clutching himself.

"What about him?"

"The coffee will kill anything he caught from Kensey."

She grimaces and shifts away from him. "What about the truck?"

"Ryan will bring Scott over after practice."
She takes another sip. Her eyes roll back in her head.
"Just bring it," I growl.
She slips off the hood and hurries over.
"Traitor."
She shrugs. "It's really good coffee."

CHAPTER 10

lying Monkey Asses

Thankfully, Lizzie forgave me for the long walk back to school from Radley Pond yesterday. We spent most of the time talking about her crush on Ryan and the ongoing debate about when he'll *finally* make his move. I suggested she make the first one, but she dismissed the idea with a flick of her hand. She wants him for the long term, and I guess that means she can't be the initiator. If they commit to each other, it'll be an enormous step for both of them. Not to mention that most of the school will be devastated that the hunky football stud and the easy hookup girl would be off the market.

I'm not sure how the closed-minded townspeople would feel about it either, but then again, Ryan's no longer the token new boy with two dads and skin a different shade than theirs. They stopped throwing their misguided, malicious gossip at him the night of the two seventy-five-yard touchdowns. Now he gets well-deserved pats on the back whenever he walks into a store.

They still keep their doors locked at night though. Believe me, I've checked.

Anyway, when we finally got back to the school, we left a note on Ryan's car asking him to take Scott to his truck. I managed to avoid Scott's wrath last night at dinner, feigning illness—which wasn't that difficult at all, because Breas really does make me sick. And this morning, since Breas rode with us to school again, Scott couldn't talk to me about it in the truck—even though he's dying to. It's like I can hear his thoughts shouting at me.

And evidently a crowded hallway before class is as good a place as any to do it.

"Why did you take my truck, Gigi?"

I pull at my collar. It's hot in here and hard to breath. And why is it so freaking crowded?

"I didn't feel like staying in school."

"You never feel like staying in school, but you don't normally take my truck."

"How do you know? You always have practice."

"You'd be surprised how observant I am. For instance, you don't like Breas much."

"That's an understatement."

"Why?"

My evil eye activates.

He swats at the air as if he's combating an enemy. "Don't even try that on me. It doesn't work."

I punch his arm. "It always works."

"Don't flatter yourself and don't avoid my question. Why don't you like Breas?"

"He's cocky."

"You've liked plenty of guys that are cocky. Plenty."

"He's a bastard."

"You've liked plenty of guys that are bastards."

I can't argue with his logic.

"What is it about Breas?" he asks, staring at me, trying to weasel his way into my soul.

I avoid his gaze.

He grabs my hand. "What is it, Gigi?"

I pull back. "I don't know, Scott. I don't know."

Ryan tugs us into a bear hug before releasing us. "What don't you know? Do you not know that I'm the best thing that's ever happened to Vernal Falls? Because I thought that was common knowledge."

I laugh. "Someone thinks a little too highly of himself."

He waves his hands in front of him. "No, no, just honest. I mean they're still talking about my sixty-yard TD last weekend, followed by two more dive-bomb TDs. Scott and I were literally on fire. Aliquippa's grounds crew won't be able to get those flame marks out until next year, and then we'll rip them up again."

"They play here next year," Scott says.

"Even better. Like when we hand Central their asses Friday night. Gi, you and Lizzie are coming, right?"

"I don't..."

"You have to. You always come. You never miss our home games."

They morph into pitiful puppies that convince me to agree to anything they ask, including the participation in archaic institutions like Friday night football. "Please, please," they beg in unison.

"I'll be there."

"And Lizzie too?" Ryan asks, wagging his tail hopefully.

"And Lizzie too."

"Yay," they clap together. Yes, two oversized football players clap like giddy school girls.

Well, not this school girl, but other school girls that get

annoyingly giddy because they grew up with a mom who made them peanut butter and fluff sandwiches sliced on a princess-cut angle and braided their hair in perfectly symmetrical French braids. Girls who had their fathers take them to father-daughter dances and didn't have to rely on an honorary next-door neighbor adopted uncle. Girls who didn't spin complex tales that would make James Bond proud. Lies that mostly relied on acronyms like CIA, FBI, and NSA. No, this school girl does not get giddy.

"Make sure to get there early so you can cheer for us when we run out of the locker room," Ryan says.

"Are you really going to subject me to that sort of torture?"

"Most girls don't consider cheering for their friends torture."

"I think we've established that I am not like 'most girls.'"

Breas slips his arm around my waist from behind. "No, you're not, Gi. You're all woman."

"I wouldn't if I were you," Scott warns him, but he's too late.

Learning my lesson from last time, I don't stomp down on his boot. Instead I lift my knee high and swing backward. When my boot connects to his knee, he cries out. I find this response very satisfying, but instead of turning around to receive more satisfaction in his hunched-over frame, I storm down the hallway.

"OMG, Breas, are you okay?" someone calls. A female someone.

My stomach drops. I know I shouldn't look. I know I shouldn't give one flying monkey's ass who's coming to Breas's aid, but I do look, and my tarnished soul might even care. Dread spawns in my gut as I watch Kensey, with her low-cut V-neck shirt, shove her exposed mounded flesh into Breas's face as he's doubled over.

He tilts his face. He very clearly sees me, and I very clearly see him. He raises an eyebrow. An invitation to return to his side and do all the things I've fantasized about. I take a step in his direction. More compulsion than anything else. His lip raises before burrowing his nose into Kensey's chest. He moans.

She pats his back. "There, there."

Mother effer.

I kick the closest locker. Nothing happens. I kick it again. Harder. Angrier. The door pops open. I rip out neatly stacked binders. I tear up organized notebooks. I shred color-coded folders. Tree pulp carcasses swirl around me as I pull out the occupant's ridiculous feather-trimmed mirror and smash it over my knee. The jagged plastic cuts into my skin.

As blood bubbles to the surface and oozes down my leg, some rage releases with it. It's the most pleasure I've felt in months. Years really. I grab a shard and slice at my wrist. More rage slips away. I swing to slice again. A white hand wraps around my wrist. Then a black one. Then another white one. Then a black arm.

I kick.

I claw.

I swipe.

Arms tense. Hands tighten.

"Get her outside," Scott shouts, his booming voice deafening to my ear.

"Easier said than done," Ryan grunts, dragging me down the hall.

"Find Lizzie!" Scott says, his voice sounding farther away.

"Yeah right," Ryan mumbles.

I dig my boots into the floor, but his meaty football-catching arms won't drop me any more than one of the pigskins Scott will throw him Friday night.

"Gi, stop fighting."

I kick.

I claw.

"Ouch!" he groans. He clamps down on me like a vise, removing any chance of movement. He pushes through the side door. Alarms blast.

"Emergency exit, shithead," I hiss.

My head knocks into the door. I don't think it was an accident.

The instant the sun hits my skin, sharp pains shoot through my knees and legs and up my arms and chest. This must be what it feels like when a witch is burned at the stake.

Ryan dumps me on the ground and jumps away. "What the hell was that?"

My fingers reach through the grass and claw into the soil. The tips of my fingers absorb the coolness of the dirt. Hatred empties from me, leaving nothing but a broken, hollow shell behind.

The sun reinhabits my body, pushing out whatever darkness sought refuge within me moments before.

"Better?" Ryan asks.

"Better," I whisper into the blades of grass.

"You've got a lot of explaining to do," a man bellows.

I lift my head. Black loafers stop in front of my face.

"Principal Donahue."

"Gigi."

CHAPTER 11

Bundle O' Nerves

Three days' out-of-school suspension. The Walrus thought he was punishing me. He spewed words like, "I hope you learned your lesson," and "Gigi, this is the last time." Actually, he paused after that one. He and I both knew it wouldn't be my last time, especially if he continues to refuse expelling me.

The reality is I'm enjoying my free school pass. I don't have to go to class—not that I went that often anyway. I don't have to eat in the cafeteria—not that I ever ate any of the food. And I don't have to see Breas. Yes, I am well aware that Breas lives next door to me. And yes, I am aware that they'll be over for dinner tomorrow night because it's the night before the big game, and Scott, Uncle Mark, and Ryan always come over for dinner the night before a big game, though I'm not sure why because we don't serve anything that once had a face on it.

But still, Gram's worried about me. Uncle Mark's worried about me. Ryan and Scott are definitely worried about me, because they unfortunately not only witnessed my little hissy fit but the self-mutilation as well. As a result, tonight's family dinner is cancelled with no unscheduled visitors, and Gram and I sit across from each other sipping soup, pretending not to acknowledge the absence of half the table.

"So, Gigi," she says.

"So, Gram," I reply.

She smiles at me, but it's a tight, tired smile. A smile that tells me she doesn't want to play games. "What happened today?"

I scratch the bandage on my left wrist. "Nothing."

She sets her spoon on the table. It rattles back and forth, sounding much louder than it normally would if Scott and Uncle Mark were at the table. She keeps watching me.

I suck in a deep breath through my nose. "Breas. Breas bothers me."

She picks up the spoon and studies the handle. An observer might think she's lost interest in the conversation, but I know better. She takes a sip of soup. "Why?"

"I don't know. He makes me angry."

"What about him makes you angry?"

"Everything."

"Can you be more specific?"

"His accent."

"His accent?"

"Yeah, he's so Irish."

She swallows. "Gigi, you and I are Irish. Mark and Scott are Irish. Mark has an Irish accent. Scott does too sometimes."

"I know," I groan, "but Breas is just so annoying about it."

She frowns. "Gigi, that's not a reason, and you know it."

I sigh. "I don't really know what it is. He harasses me. I don't like him touching me without my permission."

"Well, that is a legitimate concern. Have you told him about it? Have you told anyone else?"

"No, not really. I mean I've stomped on his foot and kicked him, but I guess I haven't said anything about it to him or to anyone. I feel things with him I don't want to feel."

Her eyes lift to mine. "Like what?"

I don't often admit my emotions, but when I do, it's always to Gram. She pulls the truth out of me one reluctant nugget at a time.

"Like I feel sorta nauseous around him."

"Like a bad nauseous or a nervous nauseous."

I roll my eyes. "Is there a difference?"

"Yes."

"Fine. I guess like a nervous nauseous."

"So, he makes you uncomfortable?"

I nod my head up and down. "Yes, yes, that's exactly what he does. He makes me uncomfortable."

"So, you have feelings for him?"

"I … I wouldn't call them feelings, unless you consider wanting to punch him in the face feelings, which you know I do."

She pulls her lips to the side in that motherly way, or I guess in a motherly way. I wouldn't know. But I imagine her pulling her lips in just like that with her daughter.

"Is it because he's very handsome?"

My eyes open wide. "Gram!"

"What? He is."

"You're like five times his age."

She laughs. "I can still acknowledge when a man or a woman is attractive. I'm not dead."

"Ew, let's not go there."

"So, is it?"

"Is it what?"

"Gigi, you are a test in patience every conversation."

"Thank you."

"That wasn't a compliment. Do you think he's attractive?"

"Well, yeah. I guess, but that's not it."

"What *is* it?"

"Well, his first day I was called down to Donahue because I was smoking in the bathroom."

Gram's eyes widen.

I put up my hands. "I wasn't smoking. I was just experimenting with smells and people. A social experiment."

She rolls her eyes. "Go on."

"Well, he walked out of Donahue's office and took one look at me and said, 'You're mine.'"

"That's it?"

I straighten. "Isn't that enough?"

"Gigi, haven't you learned by now that you can't take what people say to heart. You let their words bother you."

I start clearing the table, throwing spoons into bowls, and moving the salt and pepper shakers. "I don't."

"Gigi, I know you do."

"I—"

She raises her hand. "I'm not finished. You put a wall around you to keep people out."

"I don't keep you out. Or Uncle Mark, or Ryan and Lizzie, or Scott—as much as I *try* to keep him out."

"Gigi..." she warns.

"I'm sorry. I love Scott ... mostly."

Her eyes widen.

"Kidding. But, Gram, are you suggesting I should let Breas in?"

"I'd like you to acknowledge your feelings and decide if you really do care about him or if he's making you care about him because he's harassing you. It's not okay for him to touch you without your permission, and if I need to, I'll set strict guidelines, but like it or not, he's someone who is going to be in your life. You need to establish boundaries with him."

"I don't like boundaries. Can't we just kick his ass back to Ireland?"

She pulls her lips to the side. "It's not that easy. I wish it were, but there's a more complicated history."

"I don't understand."

"You will, Gigi. In time, you will."

CHAPTER 12

Soapy Kisses

I'VE NEVER BEEN a big rule follower. That shouldn't surprise anyone, but I always listen to my gram. Always. When it comes to Breas, I quietly disagree. Gram seems to think he has a role to play in my life, but she refuses to elaborate. I don't know why she needs to be so cryptic about it. Whenever she's had visions in the past, she's always told me in vivid detail what she saw, whether I wanted to hear it or not. And believe me, most times I didn't want to hear it. She has this tendency to predict my next bad decision before I can even think about making it. Like the time she handed me a box of condoms before I went to bed one night. I wound up sneaking out and proceeded to have sex with some random guy at Metropol. But here's the thing. I didn't plan on going to the club or getting sexed up with some stranger for my first time. It just happened. And she *knew* it was going to happen.

So, you can see why I'm really uneasy about the whole "acknowledge your feelings about Breas" thing. I mean, what if she's already seen Breas and me together? What if she already knows what's going to happen between us?

And there's that whole dark and sinister thing about him that nobody else seems to see. I guess I don't see it—I feel it.

I know, I know. Call the kettle black much, Gigi? But it's there. Trust me on that.

And what about my "conflicting hormone" thing, where I'm torn between jumping on his lap and testing that Irish kissing theory or ripping his balls off and shoving them through the food mill? What about *that?*

The only one thing I know for certain is that I'm a hot mess. A hot, freaking mess.

So rather than spending my school-free day figuring out my feelings about Breas, I dug in the dirt. And now I'm forced to sit next to him at dinner, and I still have no idea what my true feelings are, and I'm not about to talk to him about it.

Thank goodness Ryan, Scott, and Uncle Mark are over for their Thursday-night-before-the-big-game routine. They can act as a buffer.

For most of the meal, Breas has been very cordial to me. Nice even. Maybe he feels bad about what happened yesterday, as he should. Maybe he really does care about me. Maybe he really wants to get to know me.

"So, Gi, will you take me to the game tomorrow evening? I'm looking forward to experiencing America's form of football."

His fingers brush mine as I take the pasta bowl, and I almost drop it. Why in god's name do I have to feel an electric charge every time we touch? That feeling is supposed to be reserved for fairy tales and romances, but instead of making me lovey-dovey, it makes me want to break something.

I take a deep breath to steady myself. "I thought we already discussed that you do not call me 'Gi.' That name is reserved for family and loved ones, and you are neither."

"Gigi," Gram scolds. "Be nice."

"I am being nice. I'm letting him know his boundaries. Familiar nicknames are not one of them."

That's it. Embrace your anger. You know exactly how you feel about that.

"Breas," Uncle Mark says, "why don't you sit with me at the game? I sit with Ryan's dads and a few other parents in the stands next to the band. Best seats in the house."

Ryan grins at Scott. The parent cheering section led by their dads is notorious. Pom-poms, noise-makers, and two words: body paint.

I don't sit anywhere near the parent cheering section, nor would I subject anyone I care about to that form of abuse. Not even Breas.

"If Gigi doesn't change her mind, I would be happy to. Otherwise, I'd prefer my American experience to be surrounded by my peers."

Scott's eyes meet mine. It's a warning to remain calm and not make a scene. He should know I never make a scene. Well, I'd never make a scene at Gram's—that's just disrespectful.

"Gigi, I think you'll wash the dishes by yourself tonight," Gram says. She considers solo dishwashing a form of punishment. She doesn't realize it's a reprieve from the after-dinner conversation with the present company.

I shrug. "Sure. I'll get started."

Breas pulls the salad bowl just out of my reach. "Let me help you with that."

"No, I've got it." I reach for it, but he's lifted it in the air.

"I'm the guest, and I'm choosing to help," he says with that smile that's growing on me like a fungus on the bottom of my foot.

"I'll be out in the rose garden," Gram says. She nods at me before disappearing through the back door.

Uncle Mark stands up and follows her out. "We'll join you. Scott, Ryan, let's go."

Ryan follows them out with no concern for my well-being, but that's Ryan. He assumes the best in people, even when I've proven otherwise.

Scott, however, knows me better. He pushes out his chair and carries his plate over to the sink. "Do you think that's such a good idea?"

"They'll be fine," Uncle Mark yells through the screen door.

Scott scrunches his forehead at Breas. "Gi, are you sure you're okay with him helping you?"

So much for discreet. I glance up at Breas. He winks at me, making my stomach churn.

"Scott, come on," his dad calls for him again. "Let's not keep Gram waiting!"

"Sorry," he mouths on his way out.

The air shifts in the room when he exits. As if he took all the pure, positive energy with him and left raw, sensual tension behind. A shiver runs through me.

"Are you cold?" Breas asks, his hot breath on my neck. The fuzziness returns. It's like he's my dealer and the slightest interaction with him sets off my cravings.

I plunge a plate into the hot, soapy water and start scrubbing off dinner remnants. "Nope, not at all."

"Shall I rinse?" He dips his hand into the water. His finger caresses mine as he reaches for the plate. The touch triggers a memory of our lips pressed together.

I suck in a breath. He's standing close. Uncomfortably

close. So close that I could rest my head against his chest. So close that all he has to do is bend down to kiss me.

As if reading my mind, he cups my face in his wet, soapy hand. His head dips down. His lips hover just above mine. I push into his. The moment our lips touch, everything goes black.

CHAPTER 13

Secret Keepers

FRIDAY NIGHT. The night of the big game. Scott and Ryan promise it will be a game to remember. Sidenote: Scott and Ryan promise *every* game will be one to remember. Lizzie wants to go, and I had promised the boys I'd go. Technically, since I'm suspended I'm not supposed to be on school grounds, though I've never been one for technicalities. But after what happened with Breas last night, I don't want to be within a twenty-mile radius of him. I can't trust myself around him. He gives me the shakes.

Lizzie and I meet at the Quikmart before the game just like always. Her parents think she has a Friday night Bible study group, so they never question her Friday night whereabouts. It's very convenient.

I pick up a sixteen-ounce cup and dump in the remainder of the espresso. "You stay and go to the game."

Lizzie pours herself a blue raspberry slushie. "You shouldn't be alone."

"I won't be alone. I'm going out."

She hands the Quikmart clerk money for both our drinks. "Do I even want to know where?"

"Metropol. Completely safe. Completely harmless."

"Gigi, you and I have very different definitions of safe and harmless. Is Dead Bastards playing tonight? Is that why you want to go?"

I avoid her gaze by opening the door for her. "No, I learned my lesson the last time."

"I've heard that before."

I grunt. "True. But really, Dead Bastards aren't playing this month anywhere near Pittsburgh."

Her eyebrows rise.

"Not that I checked or anything."

She reaches for my hands. "Just stay away from them. You deserve better."

"I know." I sniff, but it has nothing to do with any feeling swirling inside of me. It's because of the coffee for god's sake.

"Do you? Because sometimes I don't think you do. You were underage. They should never have put you in that situation."

"I had too much to drink. It was my fault."

She squeezes my hands. "Gigi, look at me."

I sigh, acting like I can't believe she's making me look at her, but what I'm really doing is erasing the emotion from my face.

"It's not your fault," she says.

"I know."

She scrunches her forehead and looks at me. I mean really looks at me. "Do you? Do you really believe it's not your fault? They should not have taken advantage of you like that. You were underage and drunk."

I swallow. Heat creeps up my throat when I even think about adjusting the truth. "I do. It wasn't my fault."

"Then why do you need to go there tonight? Why don't you come to the game with me? Scott and Ryan will be bummed if you don't go."

"I just don't want to run into anyone." At least that's not a lie.

"Like anyone with an Irish accent and lives next door to you?" Her dimple pops up.

"Maybe."

Lizzie may have been homeschooled until she was eight, and her JW parents might try to shield her from temptation and sin, but she knows things. All kinds of things. So many things that it's almost like she was swapped out for a changeling from one of those old Irish tales that Gram used to tell me.

"So, Breas," she says.

"I don't want to talk about it."

"Okay …" she says.

"Let's talk about Ryan instead."

Her eyes brighten. "What about Ryan?"

"What's going on with you two?"

She blushes. A warm pink washes over her cheeks. She's lovely when she's bashful. It's a becoming trait on her.

"Nothing."

"Nothing?"

"We've been talking a lot these last few days."

"Oh really?"

Red blooms up her neck. "Well, you got kicked out. I had to talk to someone."

I grin at her. "Absolutely. You absolutely had to 'talk' to someone."

"Nothing happened."

I raise my eyebrow.

"Seriously," she says. "Nothing happened."

"Do you want something to happen?"

She peeks over at me. "I think so."

"What will your parents say?"

Lizzie's parents love Lizzie. They preach about loving thy neighbor and spreading the word of Jehovah and all sorts of Hallmark crap, but the thing is that while it's okay for Lizzie to minister the random unknown misguided teen girl, it won't be okay for their little Lizzie to date someone of a different race *or* someone with two dads.

She shrugs. "I don't think they'd like it very much."

"They don't need to know."

"True," she says carefully. "And for right now, I don't want them to."

"I can definitely help with keeping secrets."

"That I do know."

"You're pretty good at keeping secrets too."

She pulls back. "Pretty good?"

I grin. "Excellent. Incredible. The Bestest. The ultimate secret keeper."

"Yeah," she says smiling, "that sounds about right."

"Ryan asked what you're doing after the game tonight."

She smiles. "Really? He did?"

"I bet he wants you to go to the football bonfire."

She smiles her wide, toothy grin. "Should I? I mean, should I go? I could say Bible study went late. I could also say some troubled youth needed some religious guidance."

I wink. "That's the perk of having me as your best friend."

She pulls me into a hug. "There are a lot more perks than that."

"Can't. Breathe. Lizzie," I mumble.

Breas wraps his arms around us. "What's this love fest going on? May I join in?"

We both stiffen and pull away.

He releases Lizzie, but he keeps his hand possessively on my back.

"Do you mind?" I growl.

He cups my ass cheek and squeezes. "Not at all."

I grab Lizzie's hand and pull her along. "See you at the game. We need to go home and get ready."

"Goodbye, love. I look forward to the after-party or some alone time under the bleachers."

"Me too," I shout over my shoulder. "See you later."

"Did you change your mind? Are you going?" she whispers in my ear.

"No way. Any chance of me going disappeared the moment that Irish ding-dong pinched my bum."

I make no mention of the kiss. There are some secrets even best friends don't need to share.

CHAPTER 14

one Clubbing

THE BOUNCER GIVES my ID a quick once-over before giving me a long once-over. I've been through this evaluation before. I pull my shoulders back, not in an effort to look taller, mind you, because even if I was tortured on one of those stretching devices from the old Vincent Price movies, I'd only gain another inch, maybe two at best. No, I lift to emphasize a woman's best weapon, at least in the eyes of a horny male bouncer—although it works with horny female bouncers too. He waves his meaty hook at me to enter as he slips my ID inside my cleavage.

I lied to Lizzie. I feel bad about that, but I didn't want to admit that I had no idea whether Dead Bastards was playing tonight. I just knew that I couldn't be in Vernal Falls with Breas, because I might do something I might regret. A whole lot of somethings. I'd rather be in the South Side at Metropol and do anything I want with anyone and everyone I want without any regret.

Dieter eyes me as I slide onto a barstool. "I thought I told you to take a break for a while."

"I've been gone a month. According to Webster's dictionary, that's a long break."

He pours me a neon blue drink. "They aren't playing tonight."

"I know. I didn't come for them."

He pushes the drink over to me. "Why did you come?"

"The intellectual conversation, of course." I wink as I suck down half the glass.

"You're only getting two of those tonight, so you better slow down."

I knock back the rest of the drink. "If that's the case, I better finish them now and ride it."

He shakes his head as he refills my drink. "Make sure it's the only thing you ride."

I pull my hand to my chest and gasp. "Dieter, I'm shocked by your accusations."

He waves me off. "Get out of here, kid. But I'm warning you, I'm keeping my eyes on you."

I wink at him as I pull down my sleeve to reveal my triskele tattoo. "Do you like?"

He scratches his tatted forearm. "You are seriously going to be the death of me. I'm like twice your age. It's not going to happen."

"Never know." I wink and finish the rest of my second drink.

"I do know, and that's your last one."

"Sure, sure."

As the drinks swirl around inside me, I slip in and out of the dancers making my way to the stage. I don't like to dance until I see the singer and band. For all I care, the members could be green ogres or Satan's spawn babies, but the image of them sweating to music they believe in makes the entire experience real.

I am all about being real.

The music is loud and industrial, just how I like it. It's the reason why I come here. Well, one of the reasons. The beat makes me want to kick and throw my arms out. So, I do. I thrash. I mosh. I believe right along with them.

Smoke machines lay a haze so thick I can't make out the stage or the singers or the other dancers. The entire dance floor becomes otherworldly, and I go all otherworldly with it.

I am all about otherworldly.

Sometime during my kicking and thrashing, I notice someone kicking and thrashing with me. This isn't new. I've had many dancers join in with me. Some male. Some female. The results always the same—the two of us being real together.

But the heat. I've never felt that kind of heat before. It's all-consuming. It's stifling. It's the hottest thing I've ever experienced. Hands rub the outsides of my thighs. I lose sense of myself as I fall into this new rhythm. When he starts sucking on my neck, I let him. It's all part of the experience. And when I start sucking his neck, he lets me. It's part of the experience too. The moment our lips touch, we explode. Primal instinct takes over.

I wonder briefly if Dieter slipped something into my drink, though he never has before. And at this point, I don't care, because I am only aware of the fire this person has ignited. He makes me feel more real than I have ever felt.

"Okay, that's enough," someone says, tugging me away from my partner.

Fortunately, my partner moves with me, his lips sealed to mine. To deny me him would be a terrible punishment.

Scott pries me away from two slivers of meaty flesh that burn in the best of ways. "Gi, let's go."

"Leave me alone," I growl, pushing in my partner's direction, but all I find is empty space. I lift my lips in hope that they will no longer remain single, but my partner doesn't answer the call. I squint through the haze, but I don't see him anywhere. Not that I have any idea what he looks like, but I know what his lips taste like. I will kiss everyone in the club to find him. Although with my present company, that would be impossible. Reality fucking sucks.

"He's gone," I say.

"Good, now let's go," Scott says.

I try to fight him off, but all the fire left me with my partner's disappearance. He loosens his grip, and I drop to the floor.

"Ryan, a little help here. Gigi, why do you do this to yourself?"

I can't answer even if I wanted to. Something happened tonight. That's all I know.

Something happened.

CHAPTER 15

*K*nockout Hookups

"What happened to her?" Lizzie asks.

"I don't know, but she hasn't opened her eyes for two days," Scott whispers.

"I should have gone with her. I could have stopped her from taking whatever it was she took," she whispers.

"You know you couldn't have stopped her," Ryan says. "It's not your fault."

She sniffles. An image of them embracing warms me. They both deserve to be happy. They both deserve to be loved. Neither one of them deserves to deal with my shit. No one does.

"Ryan's right," Scott says. "She does what she wants, when she wants. No one can stop her. I blame her mom."

"Why?" Lizzie asks.

"She abandoned her. Gigi's never gotten over it."

"Your mom's not around either," Ryan says.

"I know, but I have my dad and Gram and, I don't know, people handle loss differently."

"Very," Ryan whispers.

I stretch in bed but don't open my eyes. The room falls silent. They don't need to know I overheard their conversation, but I want them to stop talking. It's one thing when strangers make fun of your life and your mom and the way you look. It's quite another to hear friends you trust talk about you. They didn't say anything bad, but the truth isn't easy to hear either.

And to answer their question, I don't know why I do the things I do. Blaming my mom would be a cop-out. She's been gone so long I don't know what it even feels like to have one. And it's not Gram's fault. She's done the best she can with the granddaughter she's been given.

The mistakes I've made, the mistakes I make, are all my own. But Friday night I didn't take anything. I drank two blue shooters, and Dieter made sure none of the other bartenders gave me anything else. But something did happen. The flash of heat. The explosion of contact. I never saw his face, but no amount of alcohol can make me forget the fire he ignited. Two days of recovery is well worth whatever that something was, and let me tell you, I need more of it. A whole lot of it.

"We should go camping," Ryan says.

"Camping?" Lizzie and Scott repeat, but what they really want to say is, "Where did *that* come from?"

"Yeah, the four of us. Maybe Breas too. It'll be fun."

I open my eyes. "Camping with Breas will not be fun."

"Well, if it isn't Sleeping Beauty," Scott says.

"Can barely sleep with all of you yapping. What's with camping?"

Ryan sits down on the edge of my bed. "I thought it would be fun to camp. We could go Saturday night."

Scott flicks a bouncy ball up into the air. "Where do you want to go?"

"I was thinking the trail on the far side of Radley Pond. There's supposed to be an old farmhouse out in the middle of the woods. We could go find it."

I tug on my blanket. Ryan's giant body pulled it off when he sat down.

"I didn't realize the city boy was a big camper."

His cheeks grow pink. He glances at Lizzie and looks away. "Well, I've always wanted to, and I figured now's as good a time as any."

"I don't know if my parents will let me," Lizzie says.

She glances at me. Sleepovers are not allowed with non-JWs, especially sleepovers with boys who might compromise her believed "purity."

"I'll have to ask Gram," I say. "She's super protective."

Ryan frowns at me. "You sneak out all the time. Doesn't she notice when you're gone?"

"Not that I want to give away secrets, but I sneak out after she's asleep, and I sneak back in before she wakes up."

"I'm pretty sure she knows about your midnight raids," Scott says.

"Well, we'll see what she says. If she says yes, Lizzie, you can tell your parents your Bible study group is going on an all-night mission retreat. Gram can be your backup in case they call."

"Do you think Gram would do that?" she asks.

"Do you think I would do what?" Gram says, shuffling into the room.

I smile at her sweetly. I don't know why I bother. She always knows I want something then, because it's completely out of character.

"Gram, am I allowed to go camping next weekend with Scott, Ryan, and Lizzie?"

"What about Breas?"

"Gram, give it a rest. It's not going to happen."

She crosses her arms. "You're allowed to go, and Lizzie, I will cover for you *if* you invite Breas."

I suck air between my teeth. "Gram, are you actually encouraging me to have a sleepover with a boy in the woods?"

"Aren't Scott and Ryan boys?"

I glance at Scott. I glance at Ryan. "No. I've never made out with either one of them, nor do I want to."

A collective gasp fills the room, followed by the four of them asking the same questions.

"You made out with Breas?"

"When did this happen?"

"Why didn't you tell me?"

"Why don't you want to make out with me?" (Well, the last question was from Ryan, and that was really motivated by ego.)

I raise my hands. "Stop. I don't kiss and tell."

Collective frowns follow.

"All right, all right, sometimes I kiss and tell, but I don't really want to talk about kissing Breas. It was a moment of weakness that will not be repeated. Now, if you don't mind," I say, sweeping my hands out across the room, "everyone out except for Lizzie. I want to talk to her, girl to girl."

Breas strolls into the room. "I'd like to get in on that action."

Gram crosses her arms. Now, he's done it. Now, she will see him for the oversexed Irishman he is.

"Alloo, Rose," he says, smiling that smile that drops flies.

"Breas, remember you are a guest, and she is still my granddaughter. You are to behave accordingly."

He and Gram share a knowing look, the type she and I share when we communicate more in silence than in words.

I don't like it. Not one bit.

And what did she mean by "still?" As in, I won't be for long? Even if he and I were a couple, I would still be her granddaughter. I doubt anyone can dispute the biological evidence. Nothing says family like DNA.

"I merely wanted to check on Gigi's safety. I understand she had relations with another male at a club and wound up incapacitated for two days."

"He and I did not 'have relations.' And he didn't do anything to me that I didn't want to have done."

Lizzie blushes, Scott clucks his tongue, and Ryan winks.

Gram wags her finger at me. "I am still your grandmother, and while under my roof, you will not sneak out again."

I flutter my eyelids and dip my forehead low, knowing full well I can't pull off bashful, but why not at least make an attempt? "Am I allowed to go camping with everyone? I mean, I don't want to upset Ryan or Scott."

The boys groan beside me.

Breas straightens his relaxed posture. "Camping? I love camping."

I cross my arms. "You're not invited."

Ryan wraps an arm around Breas's shoulder. "Sure you are, laddie. Especially if you agree to kick for us on a real football team."

Breas smiles. He thinks he's won everything. Me included.

He doesn't realize that someone stole me right out from under him. I don't know who that someone is, but I will find him. The Irish dingdong can count on it.

CHAPTER 16

*S*pell Work with BFFs

LIZZIE SCOOTS next to me in the bed. "So, what is this mystery subject you can only talk to me about?"

Ryan and especially Scott weren't very happy about being excluded from our conversation. They moaned and groaned until Lizzie physically pushed them out of the room.

Breas didn't need any assistance in leaving. He's not a part of the sacred circle, and he never will be—no matter how many times I accidentally kiss him.

"Can you get my army backpack out of the back of the closet?"

"Sure." She slips off the bed and climbs into the closet, digging through the pile of dirty clothes to get to the back of it.

"Look in the far-right corner."

She crawls all the way in, disappearing into the corner

that runs the length of the attic stairs. I hear her rummaging around until she yells, "Found it."

She reappears a few seconds later with backpack in tow and plops it on my lap.

I pull my silver bullet key chain out of my pocket and use one of the keys to unlock the padlock on the backpack. I don't know when I got the silver bullet, but I always carry it with me alongside my mace. It's my good-luck charm.

"You locked it?" she whispers. She peeks behind her to make sure the door is closed. Whenever I lock a bag it usually means it's something that Gram, Uncle Mark, or really any adult (especially anyone with a badge and armed with the ability to make an arrest) can't see.

I NOD as I place the lock on the nightstand.

"What is it?"

"Patience."

I pull out three cans of spray paint and place them alongside the lock.

Lizzie clicks her tongue. Sometimes it's endearing and sometimes it's judgmental. "You restocked? I thought we decided you were going to stop your graffiti addiction."

"It's street art, and the world needs more of it, but that's not what I wanted to show you."

I reach back into my bag. My hands tingle when they make contact with the book. I clench my jaw to ward off the mild electric current. There's definitely some creepy paranormal crap going down with it.

"I've been meaning to show you this, but between Breas and the unplanned suspension, my plans were rearranged."

Ignoring the book in my hands, she says to me, "Did you really kiss him?"

I fall back into the memory of it. The sensation of when

our lips met. His tongue slipping into my mouth. But that's all I remember. I blacked out. I could have slept with him for all I know, though I'm sure he would have bragged about it if we did.

"Momentary lapse of reason."

"More like insidious need to jump him," she grins, her eyebrows dancing. "What was he like?"

I bunch my forehead at her.

"His kisses, I mean."

I shrug, thinking about my Friday night. "I've had better."

"Really? Because I imagine he's very experienced."

"And you would know this how?"

She blushes, fidgeting with the edge of the book. She doesn't seem affected by an electric charge at all. "No reason, just a guess. There have been rumors at school about him and Kensey."

I clear my throat, trying not to think about Breas and Kensey. Trying not to think about Breas period. "I'm sure there have, but let's not talk about him. I found this in the attic under a floorboard."

She bends over to read the spine. "What kind of book is it?"

I flip it open. "Well, I'm not entirely sure, but I think it's a spell book."

Her eyes widen. "A spell book? What makes you say that?"

"I don't know. Just a feeling. I can't read any of the words, but look." I point to the Celtic triskele.

"Wait ..." she bends down closer to study it, "is that your shoulder tattoo?"

I pull down my shirt. "Yeah, isn't that weird?"

She shrugs. "Sorta. I mean, Celtic symbols are pretty common."

"Yeah, but what are the chances that the first symbol on the cover is the exact one I have on my shoulder."

"True," she says, leafing through the book. Every other page or so, she stops and studies the symbols and words. When she finds something really interesting, her eyes brighten, and she lifts the book close to her face as if she's trying to insert herself into the scene. Other times, when she stumbles upon a particularly shocking image—and the book's loaded with them—she jerks back and looks to me for confirmation that she will be okay.

I nod back for reassurance, but she should know me well enough to know that I can't make that guarantee. I can never protect her the way she deserves to be protected.

If she feels an electric charge, she doesn't show it. Maybe the tingly sensation is just in my imagination. After all, the past seven days have been one strange encounter after the next. First Breas, then I black out a bunch of times, then I find the book, then Friday night at Metropol and my mysterious dance partner.

Or maybe the tingly charge is just some flashback from a bad trip, which would serve me right for taking things that aren't natural, but I can never say no to the guys in the band. Never. No matter how bad something is for me. Especially if it's bad for me. I just keep showing up for more.

"Why do you think it's a spell book?"

I flip through some pages. "I don't know, but there's some weird shit. Like here, look at this."

On one spread, there's a mythical beast—some sort of dog or wolf but larger than any canine I've ever seen. On another, a black cauldron covers most of the left page, and an old woman is throwing straw, plants, and little creatures into it.

Lizzie points to the dog-like animal. "Is that a grim like in Harry Potter?"

"I don't know. It reminds me more of a werewolf."

She shoves her shoulder into me. "Hot, sexy ones like in *True Blood*? Because those are werewolves I can get behind."

"You mean in front of?"

She blushes. "Yeah, that too."

"Don't worry. I'll warn Ryan that you enjoy howling at the moon and moonlight walks."

"Knowing him, he'd be open to that sort of thing." She tilts her head toward the ceiling and howls.

"How did things go at the bonfire?"

She furrows her forehead. "You really don't remember anything about Friday night, do you?"

"I remember most of it."

"Really? Because Ryan and Scott dragged you off the dance floor."

"That's when things start to get a little hazy."

She pulls her lips in. "I'm sure. You need to be more careful."

"I was careful. I didn't drink anything. I didn't take anything."

She gives me those wide eyes that tells me she doesn't believe a word I've said. I hate it when she does that. I hate it when she doesn't believe me. I understand why other people don't trust me, but I try never to lie to Lizzie. It's just sometimes. Well, you know, it's for her own good. But this time, I'm really telling her the truth.

"I had two drinks. Dieter wouldn't give me more."

"With good reason, but why would it take two days to recover from two drinks? You suck them down during band breaks faster than most people blink."

"That's why I don't get it. After Scott pulled me from the dance floor, I felt …" I search for the word. It's on the tip of my tongue. I can almost pull it from my brain, and … and … there it is. "Vanquished. I felt vanquished."

She shakes her head. "You and Scott are such word nerds."

"Thank you."

She rolls her eyes and returns to leafing through the

book. "For such a bad ass, you've got an odd sense of humor. Should we try one of these spells?"

If I had anything in my stomach, I'd be heaving it up over the side of the bed. The thought of Lizzie and spells makes me sick. Granted, I showed her the book, but I wasn't really thinking about using it.

"I don't know. I don't want to cause anymore rift in the universe. Besides, isn't magic like the ultimate JW sin? Like worse than premarital sex?"

She shrugs again. She really should stop hanging out with me and my apathetic behavior. I'm a terrible influence.

"Gi, we're two teenage girls with a spell book. We have to try it. It's like a law."

I raise an eyebrow. "I break laws. I don't follow them."

She bobs her head up and down over and over. "Yeah, yeah, that's what I mean. Trying a spell breaks every law of civilized convention. We can skip school and go to the indoor flea market tomorrow and buy some candles from that witch lady's stand."

I've created a monster. A JW-turned-school-skipping witch. If her parents knew the extent of her corruption, they would never have encouraged her to minister me. But I shouldn't corrupt her completely. I do have a moral compass. More or less.

"We don't need to skip. Gram has candles."

"True, but do you want Gram to know that you need them for magic spells?"

"We don't even know what the words mean. How do you expect us to recite a spell if we can't read the words?"

She returns to the grim/werewolf. She leans in to study the image. "I don't know. You've always been very imaginative."

I stare down at the picture. "I'm not that imaginative."

CHAPTER 17

hange of Plans

LIZZIE HAD me at breaking the law. I pulled the still-not-feeling-up-to-school card with Gram before Scott had time to stomp upstairs and drag my butt out of bed. My plan was to sleep in for a few more hours, then suggest to Gram that some fresh air would be good for my soul. She's a sucker for healthy outdoor living, so it works to my advantage. I'd offer to drop off her inventory of tie-dyes and mugs to her friend Darius, who happens to have a stand at the flea market. I'd seal her approval by suggesting I pick up some goat cheese from Clara, who also has a stand at the flea market.

Scott, however, ignores Gram's instructions. He marches up the stairs, swings open my door, stomps over to the bed, and yanks my pillow out from under me.

My head bangs on the bed, which sounds worse than it actually is, but still, you get the point.

"What's the deal?"

"You're not sick. You need to go to school today."

"As a matter of fact, I'm not feeling well. I think it would be best to stay home and recover from my Friday night indiscretion." Spoken with an air of entitlement that would make the Queen of Bullshit proud.

He tugs off my quilt. I scowl at him, but he's annoyingly immune to my sour faces.

"This illness doesn't have to do with Breas and Kensey does it?"

"No." I make a weak attempt to reach for the blankets, before I fall back against the bed. If I'm too sick to go to school, I'm much too weak and feeble to fight him.

"Gigi, I know there's something going on between the two of you. Everyone knows it."

I grab the blankets back. "Contrary to your Sherlock Holmes detective work, there is nothing going on between Breas and me."

"That's not what he told me last night."

A flash of us together on the workbench pops into my mind. I collapse to the bed, a feeling of dread coming over me.

"What did he say?"

"He told me that Saturday night you met him out at the greenhouse and you, uh ..." he blushes, "you, uh ..." he swallows hard, "you spent most of the night hooking up."

That would explain the dirt on my feet yesterday.

But I don't remember anything past Friday night and my mysterious dance partner. He's been all I can think about. All I've fantasized about.

And there's been a lot of fantasizing.

"What does he mean by 'hooking up?' Did we have sex?"

He blushes again, though I don't know why. It's not like

he's a virgin. Girls throw themselves at the football team with no regard for their own actions or their non-football-playing boyfriends.

It seems highly unlikely that I had sex with Breas. I think I would remember that sort of thing. And why would he wait until last night to mention it to Scott? Why didn't he gloat about it when he stalked into my room yesterday? I mean, Gram was there, but still, he strikes me as the gloating sort.

Unless ... unless maybe he really cares about me and wants to preserve my reputation—although that's already shot to hell. Maybe I haven't given him enough credit. Maybe Gram's right, and I should give him a chance.

It's certainly something to think about, especially if I already had sex with him.

Scott clears his throat. "Gi, he didn't say you had sex, but did you? And did you use protection?"

I don't want to open myself up to a lecture from Scott. He's always giving me the "Be Safe, Gigi" speech and shoving condoms into my backpack at wildly inappropriate times. Like when Uncle Mark's reading some scholarly journal in his favorite chair, and we're three feet away from him.

"If I did, it was without my knowledge."

He crosses his arms. "Gi, what did you take Friday night?"

Why does everyone insist I took something Friday? I'm not an angel by any stretch of the imagination, but I'm not an addict either. "I didn't take anything. I had two drinks and that's it."

"Don't lie to me."

I should have told him about the whole burning throat thing when we were younger, because then he'd know I'm telling the truth.

"I don't remember anything about Saturday night. I especially don't remember doing anything with Breas. Besides, what business is it of yours anyway?"

"When someone tells me that my best friend in the entire universe, the person who is the closest thing to having a sister, is screwing some guy at a club one night and another guy the next, it is my business."

I jump up. "I didn't screw anybody. Who told you that?"

"None of your business. You needed my help, and I was there."

I shove him as hard as I can. "Leave me alone."

He catches my hands. "Don't do that, Gigi. Don't push me away."

His sadness leeches into my being. It's enough to undo me. All the anger and rage seeps out of me, leaving nothing but an empty shell.

"I'm sorry. I'm such an asshole."

"You're not an asshole, but sometimes you make bad choices."

I raise an eyebrow. "Sometimes?"

He laughs. "Well, maybe more than sometimes, but not all the time."

I pull my lips to the side in an almost smile. "That's better. I do have a reputation to maintain. Thank you for saving me Friday night."

He tugs me into him for one of his hugs. "Gi, I will always be here for you. Always. That's why you need to go to school."

TEN MINUTES later I'm dressed and clutching a travel mug in the front seat of his truck. He starts backing out of the driveway. He doesn't mention the missing passenger, and I don't ask—at least for the first three minutes anyway.

But Breas is like a rash. Just because you don't scratch, doesn't mean it doesn't itch.

"Where is he?"

"Who?" Scott asks as if he has no clue who I'm talking about.

"Breas. Where is he?"

He swallows. "I didn't think he should come with us."

"That's kind of a dick move, don't you think? Do you expect him to walk?"

"Dick move? You're the queen of dick moves. The ultimate bitch."

"Thank you, but we're not talking about me. How's he getting to school?"

His face flashes through a thousand shades of pink. "Someone was going to pick him up and take him to her dad's dealership to get him some wheels."

My stomach drops. "You're kidding me."

He shakes his head. "Evidently, her dad's giving him a loaner until he goes back to Ireland."

"He's only been here a week."

He shrugs as he turns into the school parking lot. "I guess he's made quite an impression."

"I'll bet he has."

And to think that in my twisted, warped mind I thought that maybe he had feelings for me. For *me*. I should have known better.

I do know better.

As Scott drives into his assigned spot, a motorcycle pulls up behind us.

"Hey, what's the deal?" He glances in the rearview mirror, and his face goes zombie pasty.

"What? Who is it?"

He puts his hands on my shoulders to stop me from twisting around. "Gi, don't worry about it. Let's just go."

I fight to break free from his hold, but his meat hooks are too big and strong. "What's the deal? Who is it?"

Then I see the black motorcycle jacket with a female strapped to it tighter than a condom. I storm out of the truck and past the bike, the rider, and definitely his passenger.

"Gigi," he calls out, "want to try a threesome?"

Kensey shrieks in a shrill voice loud enough for the entire parking lot and half the school to hear, "The crack whore's daughter and me?"

I slow down. That bitch. That stupid, fucking bitch. I want to pound her stupid, smug face in.

"Gi, just keep walking. Walk right into the school. Pretend you're not aware of anyone or anything," Scott murmurs next to me.

"I can only imagine what STDs she carries," Kensey says. "Besides, sweetheart, I don't share."

Sweetheart. She actually called him sweetheart. What is she ninety?

"Lassie, she's got a way about her. She's well worth sharing."

Scott pushes me—well shoves me—the rest of the way into the building. Everyone's staring again. I feel like I'm on a *Groundhog Day* loop. Harry Potter's invisibility cloak would come in handy about now.

Scott storms past the gawkers and drags me down the hall into first period. Mr. Demarest glances up. I see the whites of his eyes when he realizes who Scott is with. I'm sure he's shocked to see me in his class this early on a Monday. He's shocked to see me period. I've hardly made it to first period since the first day of school, and I've got the grade to prove it.

"Knock it off, Scott. I gotta go to my locker."

He pushes me into my seat, clears off the junk from the top of it, and dumps it on Mr. Demarest's desk. Then he pulls over another desk and proceeds to sit down. He's not even in his first period. I can't believe he'd subject himself to Mr. Demarest just to make sure I stay in class.

"We're not going anywhere," he says. "Mr. Demarest will have every worksheet you need, and I have spare paper for notes. It's more important for you to be in class. Isn't that right, Mr. Demarest?"

Mr. Demarest nods his head with Scott working the strings. Scott can persuade anyone to do anything, but he never takes advantage of his talent. He's weak that way.

"Yes, yes, that's right, Mr. McCleery."

He smiles at me. "See?"

I slouch down in my seat. He might be able to make me sit through first period, but he can't keep me in school the entire day. He's got classes of his own.

Or at least I thought he did, but Mrs. LaRoche didn't act the least bit surprised when he followed me into second period and sat through her entire class too, even though he doesn't have her until eighth.

He could get away with murder.

Brownnoser.

On our way to third period, I stop in front of the girls' bathroom. "Are you planning to follow me to *all* my classes?"

"Someone needs to make sure you go."

"You're really annoying, you know that?"

"I do my best."

"Am I allowed to go into the bathroom by myself, or do you plan to follow me in there too?"

He swallows. "No, no, you can go by yourself. I'll wait out here."

"Thank you."

I shove the bathroom door into the tile wall, and it slams shut behind me.

Scott's so naïve. He finds the good in people. It's what makes him human, or at least that's what he says. I think it's another one of his weaknesses. And while some say the meek will inherit the Earth, the truth is, the meek get devoured by the lion.

And this lioness ain't ever going to be someone's prey.

I climb out the window and land in the grass outside the bathroom. It'll be a good five minutes before he barges in after me.

In case you've ever considered skipping school, pay attention. Nothing says "guilty" more than prowling along the edge of a building. The police are bound to be called on mere suspicion. Instead, stroll down the sidewalk in the middle of the day, acting like you're supposed to be exactly where you are, doing exactly what you're doing. Teachers, students, security guards, and administrators will believe you even if you've committed the same crime before.

Kensey steps in front of me. "Where do you think you're going?"

"Well, if it isn't the class-skipping prom queen who must have a death wish."

Her lips curl in her defiant I'll-get-you-my-pretty snarl that I, alone, ever witness. "I asked you a question."

I laugh at her and the absurdity of it all. She can't possibly expect me to answer her. She should know me better than that.

"Nothing to say? Let me get right to it then. Keep your skanky, STD-riddled vagina away from Breas. He's mine."

"Does he know that?"

She puffs out her chest. "Yes, he does."

I grunt, stalking to the sidewalk. The flea market's three blocks from school. No need to borrow Scott's truck today.

"Guess, we'll find out about that, won't we?

"You stay away from him, you filthy bitch," she yells after me.

If Lizzie wasn't expecting me at the flea market, I'd show

Kensey exactly what I think of her and her threats.

But I've got spellwork to prepare for.

CHAPTER 18

iants and Eyeballs

EVEN WITH SCOTT forcing me to attend half my classes, I still manage to meet Lizzie outside the flea market at our arranged meeting time.

"I spent the morning googling at the library," she says.

I wink at her. "I thought you were saving yourself for Ryan."

"There will be plenty left for him. Trust me."

We wind our way through the aisles to the witch lady's stand. She sells candles, incense, and all kinds of cool witchy stuff.

"I wanted to find out what color candles we should buy. The witch movies always use white candles, which of course we'll get, but for real spells you call on the elements. Fire," she puts a red candle in the basket. "Water," she adds a blue candle. "Earth," she adds in a green one. "And Air," she says, adding a yellow one. "These candles will ground us to the space."

I finger a silver ring on the table. "You're really taking this thing seriously."

She throws in a stack of white pillar candles. "I really am. I'm so excited. Beyond excited. My family doesn't celebrate holidays. I've never had candles on a birthday cake," she grips my arm, "because I don't get birthday cakes. We're doing magic in all its candle-lighted ceremony."

She bends in front of the stand's glass case. "That's cool."

I duck down next to her. "What?"

"Look," she says, pointing at a necklace with an eyeball on it. "I want it."

As if on cue—or more likely, lurking in the corner, sucking on the marrow of a thigh bone, waiting for his next victim—a long-haired giant leans over the counter.

"What do you want?"

I slowly step away from him. Truth is, I want to run as fast as I can in the opposite direction. But I know better than to reveal any weakness in front of this beast or leave Lizzie with him.

His breath wafts in our direction. Rotten carrion was clearly on the menu this morning. It makes me want to puke, but it's nothing compared to his presence. Towering, sketchy, smelly, and a half dozen other adjectives that all mean he scares the shit out of me.

I wonder where the nice, hippie witch lady is? She's much less intimidating. I think maybe she was breakfast.

Lizzie steps closer to him. "That necklace. How much?"

He shakes his bushy head with his bushy eyebrows. "S'not for sale," he says in a thick Irish accent.

She taps her foot. "Then why's it in the display case?"

He scowls at her. "You can't afford it."

"I thought it wasn't for sale. Now, I can't afford it?"

She's never this ballsy. Never. The realization that I've created a monster doesn't fill me with gleeful exultations. I shift away from the counter. The hairs on the back of my neck stand up. I do not like this man or his stand. I tug on her arm. "Let's go."

She jerks away from me. "No. I'm buying these candles, and I'm buying that necklace."

The giant's face slips into a smile, or at least I think it's a smile. I can't really tell beneath the mustache and beard and layers of scar tissue. "I'll give it to you for fifty."

Because I can't keep my mouth shut, even at inappropriate times, I say, "Fifty? That's nuts."

"Twenty-five," Lizzie counters.

He closes one eye and leans toward her. "What else you buying?"

She tosses her basket onto the counter with a loud thump. "Candles."

His giant hands paw through the pile. "Planning to do some magic tricks are we?"

"We're not some kids playing hide the quarter, and what we're planning is none of your damn business."

Damn. Lizzie said damn. Lizzie doesn't say damn. My best friend morphs into something more. If I was the Mad Hatter, I'd say there was a muchness about her. A muchness that wasn't there before.

"Thirty-five for the lot," he says, "and I'll throw in the necklace 'cause I like your spirit."

Muchness indeed.

"You got yourself a deal." She tosses thirty-five dollars on the counter.

He nods at the pile, pleased with himself before dangling the necklace in front of her. "Want to wear it?"

She catches it in her hand. He lets the thick antique chain fall across her thin fingers.

"Wow," she whispers in awe.

I don't like this situation. Not one bit.

I tug on her arm. "Let's go."

"Not yet," she growls, ripping her arm away.

As if in an out-of-body experience, I watch my nails cut into her skin. I watch as four white lines begin to seep blood. I watch as the pendant with the eyeball on the front and the Celtic symbols on the back lands in the fresh blood.

"The blood vow," the giant whispers.

"Bitch," Lizzie hisses.

I stumble backward. "I'm so sorry. I'm so sorry. I just … can we go? I want to get out of here."

"And what would the lass touched by the gods want to see?" He pulls out velvet display after velvet display.

Shivers run up my spine. "What did you say?"

"Your hair. It's been touched by the gods. Has no one told you?"

His words wrap their tight, greedy fingers around my windpipe and squeeze. Everything grows fuzzy.

"I … I need to go."

I dash out of the booth, knocking over a display of hats and mittens. The giant releases a loud, bellowing, mocking laugh. I stoop down to pick up the display, but it falls over again. More mittens and hats fall to the concrete floor. I try again and again. All the while his laugh mocks me. Frustrated with myself, I kick it, sending it flying across the aisle and into a shaggy Christmas tree display. Glass ornaments shatter on impact.

The other shopkeeper comes rushing out, raising her hands in the air. "You," she shouts, pointing at me. "You'll pay for this."

I sprint down the aisle, twisting and turning through the booths and stands. The giant's laughter follows me everywhere. There is no escape from it. I feel his eyes bore into the back of my head, marking me. I keep looking over my shoulder to make sure I'm not being followed.

"Gigi?" a man's voice says. "Gigi, what are you doing here? What's wrong?"

I rush to get away, but a large hand catches me. I jerk back but can't break free.

"Gigi, calm down. It's okay. It's okay," he murmurs in a soothing tone. "Let me get you some tea."

Tea? I turn to my captor. A bright white smile greets me.

"Darius?"

"At your service," he says, bowing. "You're shaking like a leaf. Let's get you something to drink."

He gently pulls me into his stand and guides me to a worn plaid upholstered chair. "What brings you here today? Aren't you supposed to be in school?"

I roll my eyes. He grins as he hands me a steaming mug of tea that was sitting on the counter. I take a sip. The lavender hits me first. Then the lemon verbena and chamomile. I even taste the root of Solomon's seal, which I can't normally, so I know it's been steeping a while.

"Gram got to you too?"

He drags over a green chair. "I picked it up last week. She knows you sometimes like to troll around at the flea market instead of attend class."

"How does she always know where I'm going to show up?"

"It's one of her gifts. I imagine you have similar ones."

First touched by the gods. Now gifts. WTF.

"I don't understand."

"Well, that's for your grandmother to explain."

I roll my eyes again. "Right, like she 'explained' what happened to my mom but forgot to mention the drugs or the sperm donor."

Darius rises. His body grows to take up half the booth.

"Gigi Brennan, you listen to me. You will not disrespect your grandmother or your mother. You owe them your life. Your life," he bellows in a deep, rumbly voice.

I tug the box of mugs out of my bag and carefully place it on the counter. Then dump Gram's tie-dye T-shirts and socks onto the chair.

"My life? My life sucks hairy fucking monkey ass. I don't owe anyone anything."

"You have much to learn, Gigi Brennan," he yells at my departing back. "Much."

What little sanity I have left slips away as I rush out of the flea market. Lizzie can find her own ride home. She's probably still hypnotized by that stupid pendant. I know exactly what I need. I duck around the back of the building.

The moment the neon pink spray paint hits the concrete, relief rushes through me. The addition of green and black begins to sate the beast. My artwork demonstrates exactly what I think of this shit town, and it isn't flattering. I never realized how impactful a middle finger can be when it's six feet tall.

A motorcycle stops behind me. I don't need to turn around to know who it is. Tired of fighting, just plain fucking tired, I climb on and tuck my hands low on his waist. He lifts his steel-toed boot back onto the footrest and roars down the alley.

CHAPTER 19

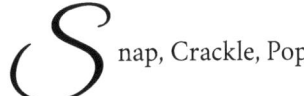

*S*nap, Crackle, Pop

Everyone makes mistakes. Some more than others. Me most of all.

Most people don't know when they're making one. They realize it later when they're eating cake and notice they used salt instead of sugar, or when they sit at their desk and the teacher hands out the unit test for the mammal reproductive system and they studied the anatomy of a fish. Well, for students who actually care enough to study, that is.

I'm not like most people. I know when I'm making a mistake. I do it for the sheer joy of the chaos it creates. The ripples in the otherwise calm universe.

As we fly past the Lathrop Honda Dealership, I dip my hands low around his waist. If there's a God of Mischief, I pray to him (actually it's probably a her) to ensure that Kensey's dad happens to look out the window and see Breas drive by on the bike he loaned him with a girl pinned to his back. A girl that is not his daughter.

Breas pushes into me. I nestle into him, resting my cheek against his back. His warmth reaches into me and down to my core. I grow drunk on revenge and something else. Something powerful—though I don't know what to name it. He banks a right turn wide, then a quick left. We race far out into the country, past strip malls, housing developments, then long stretches of wheat and corn. When he turns into a vacant lot and cuts the engine, my body hums from the vibration and a whole lot more.

He twists around so he can grab hold of my waist. The instant his fingers wrap around me, a jolt of lighting rushes through me, and all I can think about is Breas and what I want to do with him. I don't know what it is about him, but when he's around, the air is electric between us. I'm drawn to him, but I don't want to be. Tomorrow I can hate myself, but here? Now? He's everything. My fingers fan out in a desperate need to explore every line and ripple of his sculpted chest.

I've never regretted any of the mistakes I've made, but I know I will regret this one.

He smashes his lips against mine. There's nothing kind or tender or even seductive about his assault.

No warm-up. No pregame. Just get right to it.

It's not the first time I've been attacked like this. And with my "dating" habits, it won't be my last.

I suck on his neck, pulling blood vessels to the surface like Rice Krispies. Snap, crackle, pop. Snap, crackle, pop. He marks me too. Snap, crackle, pop. Snap, crackle, pop.

Revenge never tasted so delicious.

CHAPTER 20

ℒove Bites? I Think Not

THE FRUITS of my labor cover my neck. Let's not use the euphemism "love bites," because there was nothing loving about the ground battle yesterday. "Love bites" makes it seem like the two participants enjoyed themselves in a mutual marking of territory. I was too caught up in the hunt for revenge, my new drug of choice—the best high I've ever had without the pesky aftereffects—to even consider romantic feelings. Any attraction I felt for Breas, any possible feelings I harbored for him, disappeared when I climbed off his bike last night, and he gunned the engine and disappeared down the street without a goodbye or a thank you or even a parting kiss.

But today, with the appearance of my hickeys, my revenge high is back. I wrap one of Lizzie's hand-knitted arm scarves around my neck. The colors match my shirt, but the scarf swallows my neck whole. Not one hickey peeks out from the skeins of wool, and that, my friend, eliminates the point. I tug it down revealing them in all their red-welt glory.

For the first time in years, I'm excited about going to school. Kensey's reaction will make Breas's abandonment last night worth it. Besides, I don't actually know where he disappeared to. I only assumed he went over to her house, but he may have gone over to Ryan's to show off his new bike, or maybe he went to the motorcycle bar outside of town. Those bartenders will serve anyone who can reach the counter.

In my current mood, I wouldn't mind sneaking off into an empty janitor's closet or classroom with him. I certainly wouldn't resist if he wanted to do some light kissing and heavy petting—and no, I didn't reverse the adjectives. Word choice is very important to me.

Boo Bear knocks into my leg. He thinks I've taken long enough to pamper myself and now he demands my attention. Which he absolutely deserves. I lift him up and skip down the stairs.

I know.

I can't believe I skipped either.

Gram left a bowl of oatmeal with apples, bananas, and apricots for me with a steaming mug of tea beside it. She really does a good job taking care of me. I'm just the asshole grandchild who messes everything up.

Upon my entrance, she drops an apple. It rolls across the table and falls to the floor. Even the evil witch from *Snow White* couldn't save it from bruising.

"What is all over your neck?"

I drop Boo Bear, and he waddles out the pet door.

"Hickeys."

"I can see that. What possessed you to allow someone to mark you like his or her property?"

She's always been open-minded about my romantic relationships. Well, I don't know if I'd label them "romantic relationships." "Wild encounters" more aptly describes them.

I shrug my shoulders as I plop down on the chair. "Breas."

Her mouth drops open, though I have no idea why. It's not the first time I've brought hickeys into the house. Besides, she's the one who wanted me to let him in. Clearly my neck demonstrates I did what she asked me to.

After several long seconds of shock, she finally manages to stammer, "Really?"

I take a sip of my tea. She's either making the blend stronger or she's letting it steep longer. Either way I can taste the bitterness of some of the herbs. Not toxic strength, but not pleasant either. I add more honey.

"Yes, really. I thought you'd be happy."

"You thought I would be happy that my granddaughter comes down to breakfast with love bites all over her neck?"

She's so damn romantic. "Oh god, Gram, they're not love bites. They're hickeys. Proud and true."

Scott strolls into the kitchen. He sits down at his chair with his own bowl of oatmeal. "Who has love bites?"

"I don't have love bites. I have hickeys."

He peeks at my neck. "Holy crum, Gi. Who did you hook up with ...?" His eyes bug out of his head. "No ..." he gasps as if reading my mind. "You hooked up with Breas?"

Okay, so maybe he did read my mind.

"He didn't tell you?"

He turns red and shifts in his seat. Suddenly, he's fascinated with his oatmeal, shoveling it into his mouth. There's something he's not telling me, and I won't rest until I find out what.

"Out with it."

Gram points to my untouched bowl. "Gigi, aren't you going to eat?"

"I'm full. Scott, what are you not telling me?"

He scoops in the last bites of his oatmeal before jumping up. "Thanks for breakfast, Gram," he mumbles with his mouthful as he leans over to kiss her forehead.

She smiles at him; the glowing adoring smile she gives me every morning and every night. A pang of jealously rolls over me. One person in the world cares for me. One person. That's it. I hate that I have to share her with someone who isn't even blood.

She pulls me to her and wraps me in a hug to last the entire day. "You are loved by more than just me," she whispers in my ear. "Gigi, you are loved. Don't ever forget that."

So, Gram's a mind reader. I always thought it was because of all the time we've spent together, but evidently it's one of her "gifts." Whatever that means. I should go back to the flea market and ask Darius. He seems to be the expert on her gifts—and mine. I always thought I was especially talented when it came to graffiti, but I don't think tagging walls with artwork counts as a gift. At least according to Darius.

"Thanks, Gram. I love you too."

"Hurry, dear. Scott already left," she says.

I grab my bag and rush out to the truck.

"Spill it," I growl as I climb in.

He peels out of the driveway. "Spill what?"

I reach over and pinch the underside of his bicep. "Spill. It."

"Owwww," he whines. "What am I spilling?"

"Don't play dumb. You know something about Breas. What is it?"

"I know nothing about him. Nothing at all."

"Scott."

"All right, fine. I knew he hooked up last night, but I thought it was with Kensey."

"Why?"

"Because he stopped by practice and showed us his bike.

He said the bike makes lassies do crazy sexy things. Then he said he was going over to Kensey's for the evening and most likely wouldn't be home until the morning."

Fucking bastard.

"Did he come home last night?"

He shakes his head.

And there goes my revenge high.

"Did he come home this morning?"

Another shake of his head.

We drive the rest of the way to school in silence. Scott's probably thinking about all the ways he can keep me in my classes without skipping one himself, while I'm thinking about all the ways I can hurt Breas. Like face full-of-asphalt hurt. Doc-in-the-junk hurt.

And what does Kensey think? She must know that someone marked his neck. His hickeys would be impossible to miss. I made sure of that. He may have tricked her into believing he had a "slip" and somehow found his way back to her, but once she sees my neck she'll know I was the "slip."

And while she might be able to forgive an unknown hookup, she would never be able to forgive me.

The unexpected twist returns my thirst for revenge.

"What are you plotting?" Scotts asks.

"Huh?"

"You've got that look in your eye, and normally that means either the police will be involved or I'll need to drag you out of a club and you'll pass out for two days."

I smile to myself. "Don't you worry your pretty little head about it."

He clucks his tongue against the roof of his mouth—his signal that he's about to get lessony. His dad does that same thing, but at least Uncle Mark is an adult and a professor. Lessony is part of his DNA. Those suede-elbowed blazers and loafers certainly aren't worn as a result of good fashion sense. When Scott gets lessony, the result is sarcastic retorts or punches to the ribs or at least that's my reaction to him. I crack my knuckles in preparation.

"Gi, don't do anything that's going to get you kicked out of school."

"Oh, Scott, you're so cute." I tousle the back of his head. (I'd get the top of it, but I can't reach. Damn him and his giraffe relations.) "If I haven't been kicked out yet, I'm not going to unless I kill someone." I climb out of the truck and shut the door, but Scott's not through with his lesson yet.

He follows me into the building. "Gi..."

"Not that the thought has ever crossed my mind. Blood's messy, and jail doesn't sound very appealing. Too many rules to follow."

"Yes, that's what's wrong with jail. Forget the moral implications of killing someone. Gi, seriously." He stops to look at me. I mean *really* look. "Please don't hurt anyone. And please, Gi, please don't hurt yourself." His eyes water, and damn if he doesn't make mine water too. "Promise me you won't hurt yourself."

I blink a few times. "I promise," I say in a small voice. He's managed to deflate the hurt and anger out of me again. I hate it when he does that.

Ryan strolls up between us. He looks from me to Scott and back to me. "Whoa, who died?"

I raise an eyebrow to Scott, asking permission. After all my knuckles are already cracked. He pulls his lip to the side and nods. I ball my fist and swing it into Ryan's stomach. It's like punching a brick wall without the nasty gashed knuckles, but there's a tremendous amount of satisfaction when contact is made.

"Ugh, what was that for?" he says, rubbing his stomach. "You know for a little girl you pack a punch."

I stomp on his toe.

"Owwww," he squeals. "What was *that* for?"

"Just making sure I've still got it. I'd hate for anyone to think I'm getting soft." It's times like these that I feel positively giddy and forget all the baggage I normally cart around.

Lizzie rushes over to us. "Ryan, are you all right? Who hurt you?"

"Your best friend. That's who," he groans.

Lizzie turns to me. It's the first time we've seen each other since our little fight at the flea market. Her new pendant swings back and forth, staring at me. She sees my neck. Her eyes widen. Her real eyes, not her necklace. Her reaction fills me with hope that Kensey's will be far more thunderous and dramatic and, with any luck, possibly murderous.

"You didn't," she says.

I smile. "I did."

"When?"

"After."

"What's happening right now? Am I missing something?" Ryan asks Scott.

"Female intuition," he says to placate him, but he knows it's something more than that.

"Wow," Lizzie says.

"Yeah."

"She know?"

"No."

Her eyes drift past me down the hall. "She's about to find out."

The fresh scent of rain on a hot summer day shifts the air. My stomach tightens just below my belly button. I smile. I like this feeling. I like it a lot. I swing around to face Breas and Kensey, their arms slung around each other with their lips locked together.

A wave of betrayal floods me first. It strips my courage. How can he kiss her when we were together just hours ago? How can he want to be with her when he's pursued me so hard?

Or is it exactly as I've been treated dozens of times before? Once he gets what he wants, he throws me to the wolves. I'm nothing more than helpless prey.

"Confront him," a voice that sounds an awful lot like my own whispers.

"Say something," Lizzie murmurs in one ear.

"Don't do it," Scott says in the other.

"Breas!" yells Ryan from behind us.

Breas pulls away from Kensey but keeps her tucked close, as if standing apart would cause great pain. When I'm through with them, they'll know what pain is. Fear too.

"Alloo, laddies," he says to Ryan and Scott. He nods to Lizzie, then slowly—like frame-by-frame slowly—he turns to me. His eyes fall to my neck covered with his hickeys. I lift my chin to draw attention to them. He lifts his, but there's nothing there. Not one hickey. Not one mark. Not one piece of damning evidence that he was in the arms of another. "Lassies."

How can that be? I don't understand. He and I. We. My body goes numb. Black ink claws at the edges of my already questionable sanity. How can this be?

"Ewwww," Kensey whines. "Who would want to suck on Skunk's neck?"

My eyes meet Breas's. His expression reveals nothing. The jagged cut on my wrist starts to itch. I try to dig into it with my nails. Lizzie wraps her hand around it, effectively stopping me. I might hurt myself, but I'd never hurt Lizzie. Never.

"I mean, for someone to get close enough to give the

crack whore hickeys, he'd have to wear a containment suit so he wouldn't catch anything."

Scott rests his hand on my shoulder. Ryan lays his hand on the other. Their touch pulls me back to this space.

"That's enough, Kensey," Scott says.

She squints at him. "I will never understand why *you* are friends with her and the Jesus freak."

I lunge at her. It's one thing to insult me. It's quite another to insult my best friend. Scott tightens his grip, but Ryan's the one holding me back.

"Bitch," I growl.

"I hope you've all had your rabies shots, because that rodent is infected," she says. "Come, Breas. Walk me to class."

Ryan tightens his hold on me as they stroll by. Breas's gaze falls on my neck. A smile tugs on his lips, but he says nothing.

"Bastard," I growl.

It's not until they're a good ten feet away from me that I hear chanting. Low chanting, and it's coming from Lizzie.

Her eyes don't leave Breas and Kensey as she continues to chant.

"What language is she speaking?" Ryan asks Scott.

"Gaelic," he says. "She's speaking Gaelic. Lizzie," he releases me and grabs her hand, "what are you doing?"

"I think she's trying to curse them," I murmur. "Scott, you need to break the connection."

"What?" He looks from me to Lizzie and back to me.

"Break the connection. Stand in front of her so she can't see them."

Her chanting keeps getting louder and louder, growing more and more feverish with each refrain. She's almost at the end of the curse.

"Now. Do it now."

Scott steps in front of her and shakes her. "Lizzie, wake up."

She keeps chanting. Her eyes are glazed over, almost black.

He shakes her again. "Lizzie, wake up. Wake up."

Her head jerks. The black slips from her eyes and her pupils come back into focus.

Ryan releases me and wraps her in his arms. "You're okay, Lizzie. You're okay."

Scott and I share a long look. His questions form in my mind.

What was that?

I don't know.

Yes, you do.

It was a curse. How does she know a curse?

How do you know it's a curse?

Never before have his questions been so clear in my head that I can actually hear his thoughts and answer him back. Scott and I have always communicated in a way that goes beyond what Gram and I share or what Lizzie and I just experienced. I always thought it was ESP or some Freudian thing—like that sharing a crib causes two individuals to know what the other's thinking due to excessive exchange of slobber and fecal matter. But this is something new. This is some freaky paranormal shit going on.

Not that my life hasn't been without its difficulties and surprises. Hell, I've come to relish the almost-daily disruptions from an otherwise mundane world. But these last few weeks, it's been one otherworldly encounter after another, and my sanity might not break on through to the other side.

CHAPTER 21

ombie Thief

LIZZIE'S SHAKEN after the curse. Hell, I'm shaken. Scott and Ryan are hot beds of confusion not knowing what's the best line of defense or offense they should take.

Her knees wobble beneath her, as if trying to decide whether they can hold her weight or will drop out from under her. Her teeth keep chattering so hard I think they might break, and her pupils are doing a sort of creepy pinprick thing. She's not in any condition to say or do anything except stand in the middle of the hallway in a zombie-like trance. Ryan whooshes her off to class, acting as if an Egyptian history lesson is exactly what she needs to return to herself. Acting as if she didn't try to curse Kensey and Breas. Acting like she wasn't chanting Gaelic as she delivered the curse.

Two things: How did she know a curse in Gaelic? And why didn't she tell me about it?

Then it hits me.

I drop to the floor and dig through the contents of my backpack. The spell book should be nestled between my sketchbook and chemistry folder. When I don't find it, I dump the entire contents on the hallway floor. Scott scrambles across the hall to grab the cheetah-print lighter, cigarettes, and spray paint I sent flying in my mad search. I imagine he's trying to hide the damning proof that I once again smuggled banned items into school. What he doesn't realize is that if Lizzie—our dear, sweet Lizzie—lifted the spell book and was able to learn a curse written in an ancient language, we've got much more serious things to worry about than lung cancer or suspension.

"It's not here," I mutter. "It's not here. She took it. I can't believe she took it."

He bends down beside me. "What's not here? Who took what? Lizzie? Do you mean Lizzie? What did she take? Should we go get her? Should we tell her parents? Should we go to the principal? Should we—"

I hold up my hand in warning.

He immediately silences.

"I had an old book in my backpack, and now, it's not there. I think Lizzie might have taken it."

"You always have old books in your backpack. Our houses are filled with them. Why would Lizzie take an old book? What was it about?"

I flick my hand back in the air, and he shuts up. He's like a squirrel on crack sometimes.

"Let's not worry about it. I'll get it back from her after school."

He shakes his head. "I *am* going to worry about it. She was speaking in another language, and you were freaking out like you knew what she was saying even though it's a language neither one of us has heard before …" He stops and looks at me. "Have we heard that language before?"

I shove my crap back into my backpack. "I think it was Gaelic, and by the way, you said it was Gaelic too."

He nods. "I did, didn't I? How does Lizzie know Gaelic?"

"From the book she borrowed."

"I thought you said she took it. You couldn't believe she took it. If she took it, she didn't borrow it."

I narrow my eyes and shift into evil-eye mode.

"All right, I'll shut up. What should we do? Do we go get her now? Should we tell Ryan? Do I go to class? What are you going to do?"

"Scott," I raise my hand again. He quiets. "We're not going to do anything. You're going to your class. I'm going to my class, and I'll talk to her either at lunch or after school."

"You're willingly going to class?"

"Yes."

"Why?"

"I am a student at this school."

He raises both eyebrows. I don't blame him. I wouldn't believe me either.

"Fine. I want to see if anyone talks about Lizzie. I want to find out what everyone saw."

"Yeah, yeah, okay," he says backing away from me. "I'll see you later. Come get me if you need anything or figure out what's going on." He disappears around the corner.

I collapse again, taking giant breaths in and out to fight off the panic attack taking hold of me. Lizzie scared the shit out of me, but I'm the only one who can help her.

After several more inhalations, I gather my things and stomp into class. The Lizzie situation sucks, and I'm freaked out, but I can't act like I'm freaked out or these classmates of mine will eat me alive. I wear this armor for my own protection as much as theirs.

Mr. Demarest had the nerve to dump all his office supplies and papers back on my desk, which really pisses me off. I'm only twenty minutes late for class, and was in his class yesterday, and it's like he completely expected me to be at detention today or hanging out with Principal Donahue or skipping. I wish he'd at least pretend I'm a regularly attending student.

The rest of my morning classes are more of the same. I stomp in after the bell because it goes against my nature to follow the rules. The teacher runs over to clean off my desk before I can cause any damage. Then for the remainder of class, they tiptoe around me for fear that I might trip them or stab them with a pencil—I stabbed *one* teacher in sixth grade, and somehow, I can't get rid of the reputation.

Not one person mentions Lizzie or her curse attempt. Which makes me believe that either no one witnessed the scene this morning or they're completely preoccupied with my hickeys. There's a lot of speculation about the origins of them. A few even suggest that I gave them to myself for attention.

Like I need the extra attention.

By fourth period, the rumors run so wild, that even I, the girl who has spent her life listening to nasty rumors whispered about her, can't take it anymore. I turn around in search of a victim, but to my surprise and confusion, not one person is talking. They all have their heads down, working on their At the Bell assignment.

I have danced along the Cliffs of Insanity for many years, but hallucinating that I heard the thoughts of an entire class borders on a one-way ticket to a locked cell.

Is it possible that I'm really hearing my classmates' thoughts? Is it possible that this is one of the "gifts" Darius was talking about?

Because, honestly, it feels more like a curse.

CHAPTER 22

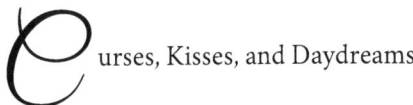urses, Kisses, and Daydreams

BY THE TIME the lunch bell rings, I'm fairly certain the constant, mind-numbing noise will drive me berserk—as if that wasn't a very real possibility already. If I didn't need to talk to Lizzie, I'd grab a cup of Gram's tea from Mrs. Paige, feign some minor medical emergency, and leave this godforsaken place. But, alas, I never get what I wish for.

As the voices continue buzzing around my brain, I smash headfirst into a freshman. The stupid, minion-T-shirt-wearing kid takes one second too long to stare at my hair, so I slash his cheek with my dagger nails. I'm in no mood for idiotic behavior. Besides, he clearly needed a lesson in manners.

As he tries not to cry, he clutches his cheek and runs away. I smile for the first time all day. His reaction makes me feel a lot better. Or at least the sight of his blood does.

I walk the rest of the way to lunch feeling hopeful that maybe some more underclassmen will knock into me. Gushing blood is a real rush.

Unfortunately, everyone keeps their distance. They've either witnessed or heard about the freshman incident (because gossip travels lightning fast) or they witnessed the witchy scene this morning and blame me and not Lizzie. And now, instead of hickeys, everyone suspects my neck is covered with boils because I'm a meth user.

Please. That shit will kill you.

As I walk into the cafeteria, Lizzie leaves through the side door with her hood up and no Ryan in sight. I didn't think he'd leave her side for the rest of the day—that's the only reason I didn't chase after her this morning. But now he's gone and left her, and she's going to wind up with a detention for wearing a hood. Detention equates to her public school death sentence in her family. By the time I reach the opposite doors, she's already disappeared down the stairs. When I finally catch up to her, I yank her arm. As she whips around her hood falls off, and I realize it's not Lizzie at all.

"Kensey."

She tries to jerk away from me, but I keep a firm grip on her.

"Get your hands off me, filth. I've got somewhere I need to be."

Just my freaking luck that I come face to face with my nemesis rather than my best friend. I forgot that Lizzie didn't wear her favorite turquoise sweatshirt today. She wore black. All black. As much out of character for her as her curse.

"Let me go," Kensey whines, trying to free herself.

I consider letting her go, but I won't give her what she wants. It's much more fun to mess with her instead. I pull her close to me as if I'm going to kiss her.

Now, a breath's width apart, I can feel the rise and fall of her chest. I can see my reflection in her terrified eyes. She might be pretending to pull away, but she's also wondering what it would be like to kiss another girl—even if it is Gigi Brennan.

Well, she's about to find out.

My lips mash into hers. The moment hers soften I shove her away.

"Dream of that, bitch."

She trips and crashes to the floor. I don't bother to check if she's okay. I can't indulge in weaknesses like caring for other people's welfare. Aside from the fact that it would ruin my reputation.

I skip down the stairs, feeling lighter than I have all day. Until I realize who was part of Kensey's lunch-skipping plans, because he's leaning against the wall at the bottom of the stairwell, obviously waiting for someone.

I should have known. I should've fucking known.

"Your little girl tried to curse me," he says with a laugh in his throat.

A throat I would like to rip out. But instead I best him at his own game. "Your little girl kissed me."

Before he can respond, I leave through the emergency exit.

The alarm goes off. In less than two minutes Donahue and a security guard will come running. They'll search for the perpetrator. They'll scratch their heads and wonder who did it. They'll remember the security camera trained on the exit. They'll search through the footage, but they'll only find a static stairwell and door without even their own captured image. And unless they realize that omission, they'll never know that the camera was altered weeks ago, just like they'll never discover who tripped the emergency exit alarm.

You'd think they'd learn by now, but unlike the townspeople from *The Boy Who Cried Wolf*, they always come running.

I, however, know enough to keep walking. I need to find Lizzie.

CHAPTER 23

ogether We Fall

THE WHEEL WAS SPINNING when I entered Gram's pottery workshop just outside the kitchen. Most afternoons after detention I either watch her form mugs and bowls on her wheel or work beside her on my own wheel learning her technique. But today, I'm completely distracted. Lizzie is all I can think about. The way she locked eyes on Breas and Kensey reminded me of one of those *Charmed* reruns. Not the good witch sisters, mind you, but the ones they fought against. The ones who practiced black magic.

Lizzie practicing black magic ... I need to get that spell book.

"Hey, Gram."

She stops spinning as soon as she hears me.

"Dear, what are you doing home?" she says, wiping her fingers with an old dish rag before tossing it over the back of a chair. It lands perfectly symmetrical with half hanging off the back of it and half hanging off the front. She always amazes me. Her natural coordination alone far surpasses any "gift" I possess, except maybe my mastery of destruction.

She picks up a Celtic knot stamp and presses it into the side of the mug. All her pottery has her signature trademark somewhere on it.

The next step of the process is probably my favorite. I watch her wind the potter wire between her fingers. When satisfied with the tautness, she places the wire on the top of the potter's wheel and drags it along the base of the mug, freeing it from its birthplace. Once it's pulled through, she carefully lifts the mug and cradles it in her hands as a mother cradling her newborn. When it's fully in her possession, she walks it over to the tall drying shelf containing today's other creations—three additional mugs, a bowl, and a vase. These masterpieces will sit on the shelf for the next few days to dry out before she fires them in the kiln.

She nods once at her near-finished product. It's all the praise she will allow herself for a job well done.

"Now," she says, rubbing her hands together, "why are you home?"

My gaze returns to the newly minted mug. "I need to find Lizzie."

She picks up the towel and wipes her hands again. "That doesn't explain why you're home. Isn't she at school?"

"Yeah, she was ..." I pause, piecing my story together, "but something happened, and I think she left."

She lifts her hand to study me. "What happened?"

After discovering my own mind-reading ability today, I know Gram can do it too. She might be an open-minded woman, but I don't think she'd be pleased to discover her granddaughter and her JW best friend were messing around with magic—especially black magic. I clear my mind in an effort to block her out.

"We got into a fight about Breas. She thinks I should go for a ride on his motorcycle with him."

She pulls her lips to the side. "And ..."

"And, I don't think I should. Motorcycles are dangerous."

The little dimple in her cheek rises to the surface. "Danger never stopped you before."

I muster the courage to continue my performance. Lies become troublesome when you veer so far from the truth that you can't reverse course even if you wanted to. Unfortunately, sometimes the truth leaves you with no choice. A slow burn forms in my throat, but it's nothing I can't tolerate.

Pulling my hands to my chest, I open my eyes wide. (Yes, the Oscar nomination committee will be knocking on my front door any minute.) "Gram, are you suggesting that I follow Lizzie's advice and go for a motorcycle ride with Breas?" I wait one ... two ... three seconds for dramatic effect and raise my voice just enough to give it the correct amount of nerves and incredulity. "With my hands wrapped around his waist?"

She rolls her eyes. "My, my, we are full of it today. Gigi, you haven't answered my question. Shouldn't you be in school?"

"I told you. Lizzie and I had a fight."

She rubs her lips together. "That doesn't explain why you're home."

"I left to find her."

"It's not your first fight."

"Well," I grab an apple, "I said some pretty mean things to her. You know what a bitch I can be when I'm in a mood."

She tilts her head in reproach but doesn't say a word, so I continue on with my performance.

"I looked all over the school but couldn't find her anywhere. Before I went on a Lizzie hunt, I figured I'd stop in and check on you."

Her eyebrows dance up and down. She doesn't believe a single lie I've fed her, but she won't call me out on it. She rarely does.

"You good?" I say.

She nods. "I'm good.

"Good, good, okay bye," I yell as I rush out the front door. I'm not sure why I actually came home in the first place. I guess I just needed to talk to Gram. She steadies me and fills me with courage when I'm not feeling all that courageous.

"Be home for dinner!"

"Will do!" I shout before hurrying out to the street.

The curtains of the "Art Thou Perfect" neighbor bunch and pool. Fan-freaking-tastic. I just supplied her with the excuse she's been searching for to lock me up. By the end of the day, the police are bound to show up after an "anonymous" tip that I wasn't in school. Luckily, Gram's quite charming. She's got me out of trouble plenty of times.

I hurry down the street. Lizzie's witchy episode this morning was my fault. I showed her the book. She was only protecting me, and now she committed the ultimate JW sin. I lied to Gram about why I was home—I hate doing that. And the reason behind today's shit show after shit show? Me hooking up with Breas. The biggest fuckup of them all. For the life of me, I can't figure out why my neck is covered with hickeys and his is clean.

Why am I always the one left dirty?

I cut across the greenway that connects my house to Lizzie's development. Rather than stick to the path, I head through the woods. When I reach the giant apple tree, I veer off to the Smith farm instead of going across the field to

Lizzie's house—more instinct than anything else. The abandoned farm is a place of comfort for me now, though it didn't used to be. According to family lore, an almost-seven-year-old me identified the well on the far side of the barn as the location of the missing eight-year-old Scott. Evidently, I'd never been to the farm before, but I knew that Scott was seventy-five feet down the well with a broken arm.

What he was doing so far away from home all by himself is a mystery to this day. How he fell in? I don't know the answer to that question either. How he fell in and didn't die? That's a miracle. How I knew that he was down there? I know that answer least of all, but believe me, I love bringing it up at every possible opportunity. It drives Scott mad that I saved him. He's always the one saving me—even when I don't need it.

I hear muffled crying coming from inside the barn. I slip over to the open door and peek in. There, huddled in a corner, is a girl wearing a black hood with brown hair sticking out the bottom of it.

"Lizzie?"

She lifts her head, her face streaked with tears. "How'd you find me?"

"Special talents of the paranormal kind."

Her eyes open wide. "Really?"

I recalibrate the lie because the almost-truth fascinates her. "You mentioned one time you liked to hang out in the barn to escape your family."

Her forehead furrows. "I don't remember ever ..."

I bob my head up and down persuading her into agreeing with me.

"... I forgot that. Good memory."

I sit down next to her. "So, what's up? Curse anyone lately?"

She blanches. "I guess I deserved that." She fingers a ripped hole on her knee. Lizzie may not wear designer clothing—it's against her JW thing—but she also never wears clothing with holes or stains. That's a Lizzie's mom thing.

"What happened?"

"I don't know. One second I was upset with the way Kensey was treating you, and the next, I was murmuring a curse I learned from your book."

"So, you did take it."

She drops her head. The eyeball necklace swings back and forth from her neck. I swear it winks at me.

"I don't know what came over me. After you showed me the book I haven't been able to stop thinking about it. I'm obsessed with it."

My stomach flip-flops. I've made a number of mistakes in my life but showing Lizzie the book may be the biggest one of all. "You're not obsessed. That makes you sound like a crazy person." I pull away from her. "You're not a crazy person, are you?"

"No," she laughs, "but the book's really incredible. There are all sorts of spells, and …" she drops her eyes, "curses."

"Curses?"

She raises her hand and beckons me to join her. "Yeah, curses too. Want to see?"

I take a deep breath. Then another. I know I should back away from the book and the necklace. Back away and never return.

It's not the spells I'm worried about. The spells are okay, but the curses are wrong and should not be given power.

But it's Lizzie. I showed her the book. I opened up this knowledge to her. I cannot—will not—leave her. I clasp her hand in mine. The heat of evil rushes up my arm. The necklace winks at me again.

I swallow back my growing reservations. I will go anywhere she goes.

She falls.

I fall.

CHAPTER 24

 ost-its and Magic

"Look," she says, flipping to a page with a yellow Post-it note.

I drag my finger along the rainbow of Post-its sticking out along the top and side of it. "Looks like someone got a little carried away at the stationary department."

She giggles, but it sounds all wrong. Too nasally. Too high. Too not-Lizzie-like.

"What do the colors represent?"

"Spells of the mind are blue. Spells of the heart, pink. Mild curses, yellow. Curses of revenge, green."

"And what do the black ones mean?"

She drops her gaze. "Curses meant to maim, injure, or kill."

Her corruption surpasses even mine. I don't know whether to be proud or terrified.

That's a lie. I'm terrified. Absolutely freaking terrified, but I won't reveal my true feelings to her.

"How did you decipher it? It's written in another language."

She peeks over at me beneath her thick lashes. "Promise you won't laugh."

I am not going to like her answer. Not at all. "Promise."

"Well," she says, "you know how there's static when you touch the book?"

Her admission confirms that I don't need to make an appointment with a therapist.

"I didn't think you felt anything. The first time I showed you, you didn't seem affected."

She shrugs her shoulders. "I guess you're not the only one who's a good actress."

"Huh. I don't know how I feel about that."

"Well, get used to it."

My *modus operandi* is violence. Lizzie is the light. Turn the other cheek. Love thy neighbor. The other day I was proud I had created a monster. Today, I am not so sure.

"Do you feel static right now?"

She shifts her seating position to face me. Her pale cheeks grow pink. "Promise you won't judge."

Shit. This will be bad. "Promise."

"It's more like it talks to me."

I swallow the lump lodged in my throat. "And what does it say?"

She flips through the book. "The words shift from whatever language it's written in to modern English."

"Gaelic. It's written in Gaelic."

She shrugs. "Sure, whatever."

"Lizzie, you spoke Gaelic when you tried to curse Breas and Kensey."

She shakes her head. "I didn't. I spoke English."

"We all heard you. You were speaking Gaelic."

Her entire mood shifts from unsure and slightly embarrassed to accusatory. "How do you know it was Gaelic anyway? The other day you didn't know what language it was written in."

Scott and I had known she was speaking Gaelic the moment she began muttering that curse, but I don't think either one of us have heard Gaelic before.

Do not tell the witch.

What. The. Fuck.

But I decide to listen to the voice inside my head and distract her instead. I select a pink Post-it note. Anything from the heart should be safe.

"Are the words changing now?"

She shakes her head. "I already know that one. It's an affection spell."

"Explain."

"I performed it last night."

"On who?"

"Well, you envision the person in your mind while you're conducting the spell."

Why is she afraid to answer my question? "On who Lizzie?"

"Ryan," she says in a small voice.

"Lizzie, Ryan already likes you."

She shakes her head. "No, he didn't. He flirted with me the way he flirts with everyone, but he liked you."

I narrow my eyes. She made me promise not to judge or laugh, but she's nuts. Off her rocker. Certifiably insane. "Are you on crack? He likes you."

Her body stiffens. "He didn't like me. I saw how he was with you the other day. The way he wrapped his arm around you."

"He wraps his arm around everyone."

"He tilted his head toward you as he guided you down the hall."

"He was making me feel better. He comforts people."

She shakes her head, refusing to listen. My Lizzie always listens to what people have to say.

"Lizzie, you saw how he was with you today. He shooed you away from Breas and Kensey. He protected you."

"Exactly. I worked the spell last night."

"And you cursed Breas and Kensey today."

She stares at me, her gaze unwavering. "And I cursed Breas and Kensey today."

The eye on her necklace stares at me, daring me to take action.

"Lizzie, you need to give me back the book."

CHAPTER 25

nife Tales

BREAS OPENS the front door before I even make it up the porch stairs. "Nice of you to join us."

I tighten the grip on my backpack. No one is getting anywhere near the spell book. Not Lizzie, not Scott, not Gram—and especially not Breas.

"Who let you out of the asylum, and why are you answering my door?"

"I don't think I'd be the one throwing stones if I were in your position."

He means Lizzie. The bastard means Lizzie. I almost drop my gaze, but I refuse to let him win a round.

"Luckily you aren't, and you didn't answer my questions."

"Mark went away on some research expedition. He'll be gone for a few days."

"That doesn't answer why you're opening my front door."

"Gram thought it best if Scott and I stay with you while he's away."

"We'll see about that." I brush past him, careful not to touch any part of him, because touching tends to make me do things I will regret later.

"Gram, what's this about Scott and him—" I growl, pointing at Breas, "—staying with us while Uncle Mark's away?"

Breas, of course, has followed me into the kitchen because he's a blood-thirsty tick.

She fidgets with her dish towel, but I can feel her hesitation before she blocks me out of her head.

"Oh that. Well, yes. They will be staying with us for a few days. Scott will stay in his room, and Breas will," she looks at him and points, "you *will* sleep on the sofa."

He clasps his arms behind his back and rocks back and forth on his heels. "Of course."

She turns back to the sink. He winks at me. He actually possesses the nerve to wink at me in front of her. A warm flush shoots into my cheeks, and then I remember my name and my thirst for violence. I stomp down on the tip of his bare toe.

"Argh," he yelps.

"Don't forget to wear your boots at all times."

Gram purses her lips. "Gigi, that wasn't nice."

A flash of guilt passes through me because I disappointed her.

"I still don't understand why they can't stay at their house. It's less than a hundred feet away, and they're both seventeen." I glance over at Breas nursing his toe. He doesn't look seventeen. He certainly doesn't act seventeen. He seems much older and far more experienced than Scott will ever be.

"Gigi, they're staying here. End of discussion."

I flinch. Gram doesn't argue with me often, but when she does, you need to nurse your wounds for a long time after.

"Who are you, and what have you done with my gram?"

She rolls her eyes. "Set the table. Or better yet, cut some new roses. The ones from the other day are already wilting."

"I don't blame them. Being forced to live in these conditions," I say, jutting my chin at Breas, "makes me wilt."

He walks alongside me. "I'll come with you."

Scott walks out of his room off the kitchen. "I wouldn't do that. When Gi's in a mood, she needs at least a seventy-five-foot radius between her and anything sharp. Step back and let her pass."

"At least *someone* respects my wishes," I yell on my way out the door.

"No," he yells after me, "just want to keep the bloodshed to a minimum. Blood stains are a bitch to get out."

"Young man," Gram warns.

He mumbles the makings of an apology, but I'm not interested in his groveling. I practically run to the greenhouse. First, the hickey situation. Then the Breas/Kensey thing. Then the spell/curse work with Lizzie. And now, Breas staying at my house.

When does it end?

Apparently with me six feet under.

My foot hooks the hose, and I fly into the air without a net to catch me. Two seconds later, I eat dirt. My hands dig in and clutch the soil.

Do not be afraid, for you are one with Earth and Beast.

I've always listened to the voices in my head, but this ... if I mentioned these voices to anyone, I'd be committed faster than someone can say, "Cuckoo's Nest."

Eventually I returned to the kitchen with a new vase of

roses, but I promise you, I took my time, selecting only the finest of blooms, carefully cutting the bottoms, meticulously dethorning the stems, and making sure the arrangement met my standards.

During the meal, Scott kept Gram and Breas entertained with football scenes starring himself and Ryan. I knew he was purposely diverting attention away from me, and I appreciated his efforts. Gram, however, was not happy with me. She made her feelings known when the meal was over and she informed me I would be cleaning the dishes on my own.

As long as Breas keeps his distance, I relish the time alone. There's something very grounding about cleaning dishes in warm, soapy water. I dip, scrub, and rinse in a soothing rhythm.

Breas steps up beside me and murmurs in my ear. "Shall I help you clean?"

My insides go warm and fuzzy. I hate the way my body reacts to him. I'd much rather knee him in the groin than fall into his lap.

"Not unless you to want to wind up in the emergency room." I plunge a knife in and out of the water for emphasis.

"You know, Gi, you can fight your desires as much as you want, but the soul wants what the soul wants."

I clutch the knife handle in my palm. "And what do you know about what my soul wants?"

"Plenty," he says, winking at me. He strolls out of the room leaving me to stare at his back. I lift the knife. I wonder how accurate my aim is.

Scott wraps his hand around mine. "Gi, put it down."

It's annoying how he always shows up when I'm contemplating doing something particularly nasty.

I plunge the knife back into the water. "I wasn't really going to do it."

He reaches in, grabs the knife, and dries it off. "Somehow I don't believe you." He slides the knife back into the block, picks up the block, and puts it in the cabinet above the fridge. I'd need a stepstool to reach it. "What is it about him that drives you to such violence? I've never seen you act like this before."

"If I knew the answer, I probably wouldn't tell you."

He sighs. "You need to think about your actions before you act. I won't always be here to protect you."

"I doubt that. I've been trying to lose you since we could crawl, but you keep following me around like an oversized labradoodle." I yank his head down so I can scratch the top of it.

"Arf, arf."

When I release him, he picks up a towel and begins drying off the dishes. "When we're done, want to watch a movie?"

"You bring *The Shining?*"

"That should be assumed, but the knife stays in the kitchen."

"You're such a bore."

CHAPTER 26

ed Rum

Boo Bear pushes his head into my leg, his subtle hint that he wants to come up. People say it's the border collie in him that causes him to nudge people. I think it's the pug in him that makes him short legged and lazy.

"Do you need some attention?" I coo. "Did I not give you enough love today?"

Sphinx claws my leg to remind me I'm already busy caring for the Queen, and the Queen doesn't share. I gently lift her and set her on the sofa next to us.

"What's with the blind animals?" Breas says.

I almost forgot *he* was in the living room with us. Boo Bear growls in annoyance, but his troubles are soon forgotten with a good scratch behind the ears.

"They're animals. Some are blind. Some aren't. The blind ones can see better than the ones who rely on their sight. Say, for example, what they think of you." I lift Boo Bear and point him at Breas. A low growl rumbles from his chest. "He's an excellent judge of character."

"Interesting. I'll remember that," he says. He almost sounds conversational, and I realize that he and I have never actually had a proper conversation. There's been kissing and hickeys, stomping and kicking, but not much verbal exchange other than barely laced threats.

Scott clears his throat. "The movie. No talking."

"Tough crowd," Breas says, winks at me again and turns back to the TV. Jack Nicholson just accepted the job at the inn.

Boo Bear purrs low in his chest as I scratch his back. He's definitely more cat than dog. Though Sphinx would disagree with that assessment.

Breas pulls out a flask from his pants. He unscrews it and takes a swig. "Ahhh," he sighs. "I needed that. Want some?" He extends it to the sofa.

"Yes!" I reach for it. Alcohol will make his presence more tolerable. The liquid burns my throat as I swallow. "Irish whiskey? Isn't that a cliché?"

He laughs. It's a nice laugh. Deep but not too deep. Baritone without the brass. "Not if you're Irish or thirsty."

When I hand it back to him, our fingers touch. It might be my imagination, but sparks fly.

He offers the flask to Scott on the other end of the sofa.

"No way. I'm not upsetting Gram by drinking in her house." He casts an accusatory glare at me.

I wave it off. "She won't mind. Everyone needs to kick back once in a while."

"Some more than others," he says and stands up. "I'm going to bed."

"But the movie just started. We haven't even gotten to laugh at the kid riding all over the inn on his Big Wheel, and you're the one who wanted to watch it." My throat burns, but that could be the alcohol.

He shrugs. "Long practice today. Math and chemistry tests tomorrow. Which, by the way, I believe you have as well."

"It's fine."

Scott's fingers skim the ceiling as he stretches. I always forget how tall he is. Then he drops them to his sides and shakes them out.

"Good night," he says and disappears down the hall.

An awkward silence follows his departure. Or at least I imagine it's awkward because I'm left alone with Breas. The whiskey's dulled the blade, but I could still make it sting.

He leans over to hand me the flask. "You want to keep watching?"

I shrug. Disinterest proves a lack of commitment.

He moves over to Scott's vacant spot. "Come on, I want to laugh at the little boy on his bike. Who's he talking to all the time anyway?"

I tip back a large shot before returning it. Heat travels to my fingertips and toes. "Movie trivia one oh one ..."

I DON'T KNOW if it was the whiskey or Stephen King's fault (he's definitely guilty of something), or a combination of the two, but while "red rum" screams fill the living room, I wind up on Breas's lap. It's not where I thought I'd end my day after his hickey betrayal, but when it comes to that Irishman, my judgment is often impaired. His fingers slide along my back as I pour myself into the kiss.

I may be one of those people who will make the same mistake over and over again, but at times like these, who wants to learn a new lesson anyway?

CHAPTER 27

*R*epeat Offender

I can't decide which is worse: the hangover or the realization that I hooked up with Breas and that this morning I will see him in all his smug glory for conquering me yet again. As I descend the stairs, each step adds to what I think is remorse, but it might be regret.

Gram sets a steaming mug of tea on the table at my spot. She lifts her head when she hears footsteps. Her eyes go round. "What happened to you?"

Scott glares at me. His anger blasts into the air like an angry storm wave. "Are those new hickeys?"

I reach up and adjust the scarf that obviously didn't hide the new batch. "No, they get darker as they fade."

They both raise their right eyebrow. It's eerie how similar they act sometimes.

Breas strolls into the room. "Good morning everyone. Beautiful day today, don't you think?" He sits down and begins eating the bowl of oatmeal Gram left for him. He scratches his neck, purposely drawing attention to the hickeys covering it.

I scowl at him. His super healing powers mysteriously evaporate when he decides to get me drunk in my house and tries to have his way with me.

He didn't by the way. I considered it. We were close, too, but just before we got carried away, I called it a night. I figured I'd made enough mistakes for one day. (I've made enough to last a lifetime.)

His hickeys are retribution. I'm sure of it. But how did he make them disappear the other day when today his neck's covered with them?

"What?" He asks with an innocence that does not become him.

"Nothing," I growl. "Scott, I'll meet you outside." I grab my hoodie and backpack and stalk out to the truck.

No one tries to stop me.

No one calls me back to eat.

No one cares whether I stay or if I disappear forever...

I should pack up all my crap and wander the streets of Pittsburgh. Gram might worry about me, but in the end, she'll understand. She'll realize that living with Breas is intolerable.

The moment I step outside the hairs on the back of my neck stand up. I whirl around, searching up and down the street for the source of my discomfort. The curtain on the neighbor's front window shifts, but I've been watched so many times by her that I don't even acknowledge her presence.

"You coming?" Scott says as he climbs into the truck, acting as if I didn't have a mini-tantrum in the kitchen moments before. I guess he's used to it, but still, doesn't he notice someone watching us?

Or watching me. I think I'm being watched.

I take one last look around. The faint remnants of cigarette smoke reach my nostrils—it's the only indication that someone other than the neighbor was stirring this early in the morning.

Scott ignores me for most of our ride to school, which is fine. I know he's mad at me for drinking last night and for hooking up with Breas, but honestly, I'm too tired and hungover to talk about it. Besides, I can't get rid of this feeling that we're being followed.

"Why do you keep looking over your shoulder?"

Yep, he's definitely annoyed.

"No reason."

He turns into the school parking lot. "Would you quit it? You're making me paranoid."

Welcome to my world. "Whatever."

He yanks the keys out of the ignition. "Yeah, whatever."

He slams the truck door shut. The cab shutters with the force of his rage. He's never taken out his anger on the truck before. He must be really pissed. Though I'm not sure why. Is he mad that I drank at home or that I hooked up with Breas again or some other completely unrelated reason?

I watch him stalk away without even a backward glance before climbing out of the cab. When I do, the hairs on the back of my neck stand up again. I twirl around. There's not one person out of the ordinary. No one who feels dangerous, because that's exactly how I'm feeling—like I'm in danger. But there's an electricity too. And this time it has nothing to do with Breas.

I hurry into school with the hope that the concrete walls will provide some safety from whoever's watching me. The second I step inside the building, I'm bombarded with hundreds of impressions and thoughts from my classmates.

Boyfriends. Girlfriends. Forgotten homework. Chem tests. I shove in ear buds to block the noise and head to first period. Ironically, a classroom full of students and a responsible adult seems like a much safer alternative to loitering the empty halls.

I forgot about the new hickeys, but my classmates didn't. Even with the music blaring, new lies and imagined misdemeanors force their way into my mind. I am all anyone can talk about. It appears that, now the channel's open, I can't change the station or shut it off.

Fan-freaking-tastic.

BY LUNCH, Scott abandons his anger with me and finds me in line. "You okay?"

I want to tell him the truth. That I'm not okay. That everyone is talking about me, and I know this because I can read their minds. Plus, someone's watching me, and I can't decide if that's a good or bad thing. But I can tell he already has enough on his mind.

"Sure, why wouldn't I be okay?"

"No reason, just checking on you."

"Uh-huh," I reply, acting like I have no idea that he spent the morning trying to mop up the mess my new hickeys created. He'd like to pretend that nothing happened between Breas and me, but our classmates make that impossible. The rumors are nothing new. It's what people do when they don't have a life of their own. But this feeling of someone watching me? It's making me itch.

He wanders in front of me, searching for a table, while Ryan takes my tray and tugs me into his side.

"You okay, Gigi? You look like you've seen a ghost."

I let him soothe me. He takes care of people just like Scott. That's what bonds them together. It's not the football muscle. It's not the rousing testosterone at pep rallies. It's this basic primal need to care for others.

"Just tired," I whisper.

"Scott told me you and Breas got drunk. I can't believe you drank at your gram's. You've never done that before."

"Ryan, there's a lot you don't know about me. I'm not a good person."

He pulls me closer. "You can keep telling yourself that, Gigi, but the ones closest to you know the truth."

Normally, this would be the time for me to crush his foot or elbow him in the stomach, because he's getting too touchy-touchy with his feelings, but contrary to popular belief, I don't like to hurt the ones I care about.

Kensey slithers next to Ryan. "Don't tell me you're hooking up with this skank whore. You can do so much better. You *have* done so much better."

He keeps me tucked in. "We all make mistakes, Kensey."

She gasps and stomps away. The buckles on her motorcycle boots clank with every step.

"Looks like someone went shopping at the bike shop," Ryan says, as we watch her black leather body disappear around the corner.

I tsk-tsk because, really, what else can I do? "Her boots are hideous and loud. She'd never be able to sneak in and out of a house with that footwear."

He nudges me. "That's my Gi. Always thinking exit strategy."

Lizzie stops in front of us. We were so busy watching Kensey, we didn't even notice her.

"Everything all right here?" she says.

I smile at her, but she doesn't return the greeting. She crosses her arms instead. I think back to our conversation yesterday and her claim that Ryan liked me more than her. She's so twisted inside her head. Maybe that's what love does to a person. Ryan's crazy about her—even without her stupid love spell. He's just afraid to make a move on her because they've been friends for so long and he doesn't want to ruin their friendship. But I know what they both want.

I lift Ryan's arm off me and place it across her shoulders. "He was trying to make me feel better. He succeeded. Now, I'll leave you two alone. Don't do anything I wouldn't do."

Ryan pulls her close to him. "That leaves a lot of room for opportunity."

"You're welcome," I nod at them before disappearing out the closest door and up the nearest stairwell, acting as if I don't have a care in the world. As if I don't have a thousand-pound weight wrapped around my neck. As if my best friend with that stupid eye necklace wasn't thinking about cursing me. I may not always get a clear read on her thoughts, but I certainly know she was deciding what curse to use on me.

When I'm far away from prying eyes, I collapse against the wall. Thank the gods that the good students of Vernal Falls have hurried themselves off to their next class. There's relief in the silence. I take deep breaths in and out and try not to think about Lizzie and what she wanted to do with me. The panic attack claws at my chest. I push my breaths in and out. In and out. I am not ruled by my fear. I am not ruled by my worry. I am in control of the situation. In and out. In and out.

When the risk of hyperventilating is over, I rest my cheek against the cold concrete block to steady myself. The air shifts. The hair on the back of my neck springs up. Someone else is here.

I glance up at the camera Donahue installed a few months back after complaints of cigarette smoke in the stairwells. The live feed plays on one of the monitors in the back corner of his office. At least if something happens to me, they'll have it on film, because I haven't had a chance to alter this camera yet.

I slide over to the railing. My boots aren't loud and clunky like Kensey's. They're built for utility and stealth. I peek over the rail.

"Hello?" I call out in a much smaller voice than I intend. The type of voice that will ruin my reputation. I try again, hoping I sound more confident. "Hello? Is anyone there?"

No one answers. I stand back up and concentrate. Thoughts come to me jumbled, like I'm listening to an FM radio and I'm just out of range. I slip down two steps. The thoughts tune in but still aren't clear. I creep down two more. I've never tried to eavesdrop on anyone's thoughts before.

My heart's pounding so hard it's making it difficult to concentrate. I can't tell if it's a male or female. I take a deep breath, trying to pick up the scent.

A fresh breeze replaces the stale hall air. The edges of my vision go soft. It's like the day Breas came to school and I passed out.

If it's Breas following me, I'm going to kick his ass. I slip down four more steps and really try to tune in, but the thoughts don't make sense. More impressions and smells. The moon. My face. Dancing in the haze. My face. Breas and I making out. My face.

"Psycho stalker!" I scream, leaping the final steps. I land and twist to confront Breas, but he's not there. No one's there. The landing's empty.

I sprint into the hall. Not a soul in sight. Not even the echo of footsteps.

Whoever's following me isn't getting away with this. That I promise.

The alarm goes off when I leave through the emergency exit. I'm pissed because my stalker can come and go without setting off the alarms—I've been trying to do that for years. And now Donahue and a security guard will come running to find out who illegally left the building, because even though there's a camera, it's not trained on the door.

I catch a hint of smoke. I whirl around. In the far distance behind a giant oak tree, there's someone standing there. I can just make out the edge of his black leather jacket. Then he's gone.

He made sure he was close enough to keep an eye on me, but far enough away that he wouldn't get caught.

I'm not scared. Though maybe I should be. All my instincts tell me I should be, but my instincts are not always very reliable.

Something tells me I just discovered my mysterious dance partner. I just need to decide if he's a murderous psycho stalker or something else.

CHAPTER 28

 ead Man's Curve

GRAM'S FORGIVEN Breas for giving her granddaughter hickeys. She's not entirely happy with me. Evidently, I should know better, or at least shouldn't prance around with my neck on display. Scott's come to grips with us hooking up. He doesn't approve, but he's decided to let the shit show stage its own production. He thinks I'll grow bored with Breas, and Breas will shuffle back to Kensey, which is probably true.

Mind you, none of this conversation was spoken aloud. I feel a little guilty about creeping in on their thoughts, but I mean, if you had a mind-reading ability, wouldn't you use it? Besides, I didn't put my ideas in their heads. I only read theirs.

Throughout dinner, the four of us are all very civil to each other. Scott and Breas entertain us with stories about Breas's first football practice. Evidently, he's quite the place kicker. We laugh. We smile. It's weird but nice that we're all getting along without me wanting to stab Breas with a fork.

After dinner, Scott washes the dishes, and we dry them. When everything's all cleaned up, Breas turns to Gram and says, "Miss Rose, may I take your granddaughter for a ride this fine evening?"

And that's when the trouble begins.

I sigh in exasperation. "Shouldn't you ask me first?"

"Of course, I know you'd like to go with me, but we need your grandmother's permission." He raises his hand palm up as he bends at the waist in front of Gram. In his own mind, he's quite the charmer.

And while at times I do find him irresistible and, as Lizzie once called him, a delicious piece of man-flesh, I don't like to be told what to do. "Motorcycles are dangerous."

Scott snorts. "You're so full of BS, Gigi."

Gram puts her hand on her hip. "Mind your language, young man."

Scott ducks his head. "I'm sorry, Gram."

"Now," she says, "Gigi, are you really going to use that excuse again? Didn't we talk about that the other day?"

Before I can come up with a satisfactory retort, she continues, "That lie didn't work when you tried to cover up the 'real' reason you and Lizzie fought, and it's not going to work now."

She knows? Scott thinks, broadcasting his thoughts loud and clear in my mind. Much different than the mixed channel from this afternoon when I received images instead of thoughts, like a TV station trying to capture a radio frequency.

No. I shake my head. By physically acknowledging his question, I feel human instead of some freak who can read minds and project thoughts.

If Gram knew about the spell book or that Lizzie was

practicing black magic she'd be pissed. She hid that book for a reason. Probably because of the curses and what they can do to people.

Breas, oblivious to the internal conversation going on between Scott and me, bows before me. "Gigi," he says, offering his hand, "may you do me the honor of going for a ride this fine evening?"

"I don't—" I start to say, but Scott interrupts me.

"You know you want to go. Stop using the danger element as a cop-out. You're not kidding anyone."

"But Gram still needs help filling the kiln."

"I'll help her," he says.

Gram pats his arm. "It won't take long anyway. Besides, Scott and I need time to chat."

"It's a sign, Gig," Breas says, leading me out the door.

"A sign of what?"

"That you should go for a ride—it's been written in the stars."

I roll my eyes and point to the setting sun. "The stars aren't even out yet."

He shrugs as he tosses me a helmet. The foul thing reeks of some sweet flowery perfume that has never touched my body.

"Ridden with anyone else lately?"

He pulls his hand to his chest, pretending to be aghast. He's in full form tonight. "Gigi, how could you accuse me of such a thing."

"Don't lie. It doesn't become you."

He juts out his chin. "But it becomes you."

"What's that supposed to mean?"

"You lied to Gram about Lizzie cursing me."

I shove my finger into his chest. "First off, she is *my* gram, not yours. You switch between 'Gram' and 'Miss Rose' depending on what suits you. She's *my* gram period." He tries to argue but I jab my finger in deeper. "Second, if you ever combine the words 'Lizzie' and 'curse' in the same sentence again, I will break your arm." He almost snorts, but the edge of a strategically pointed fingernail stops him. "Third, you need to pick Kensey or me, because I don't play sloppy seconds to anyone, especially to that bitch."

He steps closer. With blood racing through my veins, I try to catch my breath. My threats don't faze him. If anything, they've turned him on. He presses against me. My instincts tell me not to. My brain screams, "Don't do it," but that other part, that base primal part, wants to yank his lips to mine and cause the neighbor to abandon her Bible study for the rest of the evening.

"You know you want me," he murmurs as if reading my mind, but so far as I know, I'm the only one here who can do that. He edges closer. The space between us grows nonexistent. A needy burn blossoms in my chest. I lift my arms and jerk him to me. He covers my mouth with his, pushing his tongue in and out. It's not gentle. It's not seductive. I let him kiss me for several long minutes before I yank away and tug on the helmet. My patchouli essential oil will overpower the cheap perfume.

"Let's ride," I growl.

He revs the engine as he lifts his boot and takes off down the road. We chase the last remnants of the day together.

Today. At this moment. We are perfect.

But the moment won't last.

It never does.

He banks a left to Radley Pond and revs the engine again. The bike flies down the road, ever increasing its speed. He drives with the careless, reckless abandon of someone who thinks he is invincible. As if the entire world is crumbling behind us and we need only to hit the next bend, and we will be free. It's thrilling and amazing and absolutely terrifying.

I clutch his waist tighter as a silent plea to slow down. It only encourages him to go faster.

Deadman's Curve approaches at an alarming speed. The cliché will soon become our reality if he doesn't slow down. I strum my fingers against his stomach. He hits the throttle in response.

"Slow down!" I scream.

He doesn't hear me, or he ignores my plea.

"Slow down! Slow down!" I scream again and again.

Still no response.

"Breas! Slow down!"

In answer, the bike goes faster.

I squeeze tighter and scream again to stop, but he doesn't stop, and he doesn't slow down. He wants to kill us.

My god. He will kill us.

The giant pine on the hairpin curve waves to me. "Join me," it says. "You'll like it here."

But I'm not ready to die.

I've only begun to live.

Somehow he navigates the curve. I don't know how he did. All I know is that we didn't die. I'm glad we didn't. Fuck that. I'm fucking amazed we didn't.

He pulls up to the boulder overlooking Radley Pond.

As soon as he cuts the engine, I leap off the bike, stumbling to catch my footing. "Are you freaking nuts? Were you trying to kill us?"

His eyes shine bright in the dusk light, drunk on the adrenaline coursing through our veins at the near-death experience. He climbs off the bike, his legs strong. The ground bends to his will. He stalks over. Expectant of my praise. Expectant our high will join us as one.

I backpedal away from him. "You're nuts, you freaking psycho. Get away from me."

He narrows his eyes. I can't read his mind, but I know what he wants. I've seen that determination in many eyes before. He will not be diverted.

Fear crawls up my spine. He will not overpower me. Not tonight. Not ever. I will not allow that to happen again. Ever again. Swallowing my nerve, I reach into my pocket and withdraw the black canister. I flick the red switch.

"How lucky do you feel?"

"Mistake," he snarls and backs away. His eyes bore into mine before he gets back on his bike and disappears into the night.

I sway back and forth with the can of pepper spray. When the bike roars out of hearing range, I collapse. The fear, the panic, the adrenaline, all rush out of me in one mighty exhale, leaving me without even the ability to stand. Crickets lull me to sleep on a bed of soft grass.

An image of me fighting with Breas pops into my head. First at my house. Then here, along the banks of Radley Pond. I stretch my mind to read the channel, but the effort further exhausts my already weakened state. I become aware of a heat source, but I don't possess the strength to do anything about it.

As whoever approaches, my vision blurs. My thoughts too. I must be dreaming. Arms cradle me to a chest radiating with heat. Just before everything goes black, I project out, "I've only begun to live."

CHAPTER 29

New Channels and Seances

A PILLOW KNOCKS into the side of my head.

"Rise and shine, sleepyhead," Scott (a.k.a. Mr. Annoying) yells cheerfully from the foot of my bed.

I clutch the blankets to my chest, the habit so familiar I almost forget that I didn't fall asleep in my room last night.

I jerk up. How did I get into my bed?

His brow furrows. "Everything all right?"

"Yeah, just give me a minute."

"You've got ten. Don't waste them."

"Whatever."

When he closes the door behind him, I fling off my covers and leap out of bed. My sheets are covered with dirt and grass. My jeans are even still damp.

Last night wasn't a dream. It really happened. The hair on the back of my neck stands up. I hurry to the window. There, in the distance, behind a large oak tree, is the same figure I saw yesterday after the stairwell incident. He takes a long drag of his cigarette. The smoke spirals around him, clouding his presence.

"Gigi, I'm leaving in five," Scott yells from downstairs.

"Coming," I shout back. I turn back to the window. The figure is gone.

Creepy stalker turns protective guardian angel. Now, that's an interesting turn of events.

I'm not even that upset with Breas. If he didn't have his psychotic break, I would never have discovered the true nature of the person following me. I hurry to get dressed, looking forward to the prospect that my guardian angel will follow me to school again.

THE CAR RIDE WAS UNEVENTFUL. So were my morning classes —even the ones I skipped and spent in the stairwell. No special visitors, no cigarette smoke, no leather jacket in the far-off distance. By the time fourth period rolls around, I'm distracted enough that a cluster of freshmen on their way to lunch crashes into me and knocks me over. I hiss, and they scatter like marbles, leaving paper trails behind them. I've been neglectful of my duties these past few weeks. I glare around the near-empty hall, daring anyone to fight, but only one person would willingly put herself in harm's way.

Kensey rests against a locker, picking at her fingernail. "Funny they didn't move out of the way. Almost as if you didn't exist."

One thing I'll admit Kensey is good at—she always goes for the low blow. But so do I.

"That's how your boyfriend acted last night on my front lawn."

Her arms tighten into toothpicks. "You keep away from him."

A Joker smile crosses my face. "I think you should be telling your boyfriend to keep away from me. He's the one who keeps showing up at my doorstep."

She gasps. "Only because he feels sorry for you and your crack whore mom."

She makes me laugh. She really does. "You know, Kensey, it used to bother me when you said stuff like that, but now it's just white noise. Everything that comes out of your mouth is white noise."

"Well ..." she yells at my disappearing back, "well, at least I'm not a skank."

I turn around and rush at her. She backpedals, covering her face in case of a frontal attack, but I'm not going to cut her. No. Mental warfare is far more powerful and potentially more devastating.

"If I were you, I'd stop at Planned Parenthood and schedule an exam. I'd hate for you to catch *everything* I have."

The whites of her eyes turn a glaring shade of putrid. Gasping, she scurries off to the office.

To commemorate my win, I withdraw a black, chisel-tipped Sharpie from my backpack. The students of Vernal Falls should witness Miss Cheerleader Prom Queen in a tissue paper gown tagged with a self-deprecating speech bubble coming out of her mouth.

You can make donations at the "Gigi Brennan, Awesome Artist" GoFundMe site.

The Sharpie squeaks and pulls across the large picture of the cheerleading captain. Not loud enough to lure students out of their classes to watch live art, but distracting enough that I almost miss the whisper of footsteps down the hall. I add the finishing touches to my artwork before capping the marker.

I concentrate on the mind of my fellow class-skipping comrade. I'll admit, in the beginning I was hesitant about reading other people's thoughts. I mean, my thoughts are scary enough. But now I have decided to embrace my gift. My personal history has been broadcast throughout the school since the second grade. It's my turn.

I catch impressions of two people. One is Lizzie—I'd know her mind anywhere. She stole the spell book again, though I don't know how she found it. I hid it in the greenhouse under a crate of lily bulbs. She's barely ever been in the greenhouse. Everyone knows it's off-limits with the exception of Gram and occasionally Scott. It's my private sanctuary away from the real world, and she broke it.

From what I can tell, she has no intention of performing a sweet little séance with the other person. She's got something dark and tragic in mind for the girl who was supposed to call her mom and get checked for STDs at Planned Parenthood. Somehow she persuaded Kensey to go up to the school attic with her.

I don't think she's ever been up there before, though I did tell her how to open the locked door. I slip through the door and relock it behind me. Whatever she has in mind, she doesn't want to be disturbed. I climb the stairs quietly, going more by feel than sight.

Lights flicker against the walls at the top of the stairs. It appears she's brought her new witchy spell candles with her.

Their thoughts are racing so fast I can't get a read on either of them. Kensey made Lizzie snap. That much I can tell. It doesn't surprise me. That psycho whore is the root of all evil, and Lizzie wants to make her pay. She also knows I'm here.

"Hi, Gi, I was hoping you'd stop by," she says in a relaxed voice that sounds nothing like the best friend I've known for most of my life.

When I reach the attic, I am in no way prepared for the sight before me. Kensey's bound to the floor with a rough chalk pentagram around her surrounded by candles. Her eyes shoot to mine, her terror unmistakable.

"You were?" I ask.

Lizzie kneels over Kensey, flinging handfuls of salt across the floor as she chants. The singular focus of her mind leaves no room for outside interference. I need to proceed with caution, and that worries me. Caution's not my strong suit—it's Lizzie's.

"Sure, I wanted my powerful best friend with me while I take care of the trash."

"What do you mean by powerful?"

She shakes her fist at me. "Don't play games, Gigi. It doesn't suit you. You read minds, project your thoughts. You captivate guys and girls. You cast magic on those around you. You are from the Otherworld." The eye on her pendant winks at me.

I know at once what her problem is. Gram told me about a woman who couldn't touch anything once owned by someone else—furniture, jewelry, clothing, houses—because the spirit of the previous owner would appear before her. The spirits never meant her harm until the time she sat on the steamer trunk of a serial killer. From sunset to daybreak he haunted her, harassed her, tried to kill her and add her to his trophies—Freddy Krueger come to life. She wound up in a psychiatric hospital for two years until a priest performed an exorcism on her upon the request of the only person who believed her: a nurse who happened to be Gram's friend.

Either Lizzie bears the same type of curse, or that necklace is some sort of portal.

"Lizzie, can I wear your necklace?"

She grasps the blinking-eye pendant. "It's mine. I paid for it."

"I know, but we share *everything*."

"Not this. You can't have it."

"Lizzie, I don't want it. I just want to try it on." Then smash it with a hammer.

"No. Now, if you don't mind …" she says and begins chanting.

"What are you trying to do to Kensey?"

She stops to answer me, but she doesn't take her eyes off Kensey. "I've always wondered about the ability to possess someone. I wanted to see if I could do it."

"Really? Since when?"

She shrugs. "I don't know. In church there are always conversations about the possessed. I figured someone had to be the possessor. Why not me?"

My stomach churns. This day is not turning out anything like I expected. "How did you find my book?"

She snorts. "Gigi, I think we both know it's not your book. You don't appreciate it. You don't use it properly."

"I hid it. How did you find it?"

She strokes the sides of the pendant. "You're not that creative in your hiding spots."

"Why Kensey?" I glance down at her now-still frame. The slight rise and fall of her chest is the only indication that she's alive. Her eyes were open before. Why are they closed now? Did she pass out from shock? Lizzie must have already begun the spell, or curse, or whatever she's trying to do.

"We both know why."

"How'd you get her up here? She was leaving for the doctor's."

"She's very trusting of good church girls," she says, laughing a terrible, high-pitched shriek I've never heard before. "I told her Breas was up here."

"Can you take her out of the spell?"

"I could, but where's the fun in that?"

Something is seriously wrong with my best friend.

"Lizzie, let Kensey go, and we'll find Ryan. Maybe he'll skip class and hang out with us the rest of the day."

She drapes herself across the spell book as if lounging on the chaise in her room. "I'm having a lot of fun."

"Ryan's more fun. We can plan our camping trip for this weekend."

She shrugs. "I'm losing interest in Ryan. He's so good, so handsome—it's boring. I want someone, I dunno, meatier. Someone like Bre—"

But before she finishes his name, the candles blow out. Never one to miss an opportunity, I snap off her necklace. A charge surges through my hand, but I clench it tight. No way in hell is Lizzie getting a hold of it again. I shove it down my shirt.

The room fills with screams. Lizzie's, mine, Kensey's—all of us. A flash of movement. A familiar presence. Then nothing except blackness and our gasping breaths.

Lights flood the space. The brightness temporarily blinding us. "Gigi? Lizzie?"

"Scott?" Lizzie and I whisper staring at each other.

The stairs creak as he climbs up.

"How did I get here?" Lizzie whispers.

"You don't know?"

"No," she says, rubbing the side of her head. "Ugh, my head is killing me." She stops to look around. "Where are we anyway?"

The steps keep getting louder. I'd like to find out how he unlocked the door, but there's no time for inquisitions. He'll be here in less than a minute, and I need to get rid of the evidence of Lizzie's spell work. Scott is understanding about a lot of things, but he won't let this pass. I reach over to untie Kensey, but here's the thing ... she's gone. Her bindings, the pentagram, the candles, the spell book. All gone. I jump up, searching the dark corners of the room. No Kensey, no candles, nothing. I race to the other storage areas, my heart pounding in my chest. A person doesn't just disappear. She's got to be here somewhere. I drop to my knees in front of Lizzie, resting my hands on her thighs.

"Lizzie, you don't remember anything?"

"No," she sighs, her hand returning to her head. "My head's killing me."

Scott rushes over to us. "What are you doing here?"

"I can ask you the same thing," Donahue roars from the bottom of the stairs.

The pendant moves against my skin as if winking.

CHAPTER 30

*L*ies and Misdemeanors

NOTHING about what happened in that attic makes sense. Not Lizzie's behavior. Not the séance. Not Kensey's disappearance.

"I'm going to ask you one more time," Donahue barks from the other side of his desk, "what were you doing up in the attic?"

"I was looking for them," Scott says. "I didn't know where Gigi was."

"You," Donahue says, pointing at Lizzie who hasn't stopped clutching her head. "What were you doing up there with The Delinquent?"

She begins to shake again. She's barely stopped since Scott and Donahue found us.

"Can she get something for her headache?" I growl.

"After she answers my question."

Her wide eyes beg me for help. She's never been in the principal's office before. She's never been in trouble before. If I have my way, she never will be again.

"Can't you see she needs to go home? She's a mess. She can't even hold up her head."

He glances at her and swallows, then crosses his arms over his massive chest. "No. Not until she answers my question."

What little color returned to her seeps out of her cheeks. My Lizzie is fading away before my very eyes. I can stop it. I can stop all of it.

"Fine," I snap. I swallow to prepare my throat. "I'll tell you."

The pendant vibrates, almost whispering, "Yes, that's it."

"I wanted some privacy with Lizzie." My throat itches from the partial truth.

"Why?" he says.

"I wanted to show her my new tattoo."

He blows out his nose. It's times like these he reminds me more of a bull than a walrus. "You couldn't show her your tattoo in the bathroom?"

I can feel Scott and Lizzie's gaze. They don't know whether to believe me or not. They want to believe me. That much I know. And I want them to believe me. No one needs to know what really happened in that attic, because to be honest, I'm not even sure myself. I need to sell the lie even if my throat lights on fire. "It's in a very private area."

I wait for the burn but it's not as strong as I thought it would be. I do have a new tattoo—I got it before I went to Metropol last Friday, but it's below my left breast. A semi-private area depending on the outfit.

Donahue clears his throat. "And a bathroom stall wouldn't work because …?"

He puts me in a tight spot. Lizzie and Scott know I lie a lot. They even suspect I've lied to them on occasion, but they don't know for sure. I can't say I've never lied to them, but I do my best not to. They're both trying to figure out if I'm lying to Donahue.

"It's in a really private area, and the bathroom stall would be too tight. I couldn't risk anyone coming in and seeing me —" I bring my hand to my chest "—*naked.*"

Donahue blushes. Lizzie and Scott blush too. They know I got another tattoo, but they don't know where it is. Only Breas has seen it.

"Principal Donahue, I know that I often get in trouble because I make bad choices, but that's not Lizzie's fault. Please don't call her parents. Call my gram if you must, but please don't call hers."

"I really—" he says, but Scott interrupts.

"Principal Donahue, I saw an old mascot uniform in the attic. Any chance we could use it for the pep rally next week?"

Donahue blinks as if a switch was flipped, and I'm pretty sure Scott's working the controls. He's always been good at persuading people to do what he wants, but I've never witnessed it used with such success. I mean, Donahue was a bloodhound hot on the tracks of the truth, and now he's completely distracted with the prospect of new mascot outfits.

"I don't see why not. Let's go back up and take a look," he says. "Lizzie and Gigi, you may go, but if I catch you upstairs again, there will be serious consequences, and your parents will be called."

Scott winks at me as he leaves with Donahue. I grab Lizzie's hand and help her stand up. Color begins to return to her cheeks. I guide her out of his office. Maybe all she needs is a little rest.

Mrs. Kelso offers us her bowl of Peppermint Patties. "Gigi, I haven't seen you for an entire week. It's boring without you."

My mouth waters as I unwrap my black-foiled Pattie. I'm a Peppermint Pattie addict, and Mrs. Kelso's my supplier.

"Don't worry, I've given Donahue a lot to think about. He'll probably seek your counsel soon."

"You must have handed him a doozy."

Ryan bursts into the office. "There you are. I've been searching everywhere for you. Scott said he left you in here." He wraps Lizzie into an embrace. "Do you feel okay? You look pale."

And she does. Whatever color crawled back into her cheeks while we were holding hands left as soon as she let go of mine.

Her knees drop out from under her. Ryan swoops her into his arms. Her head falls against his chest.

"Should I call an ambulance?" Mrs. Kelso calls to us.

I check her forehead. It's ice cold. Traditional medicine won't touch what she has. "She needs Gram's tea. Ryan, get her to your car. I'll be right there."

"Herbal tea? Really?" Mrs. Kelso says. "I could just call …"

I rest my hand on hers. "Lizzie's going to be okay."

She nods with me.

"Please let Scott know we went to Gram's house."

She nods again.

"Don't let Donahue find out."

"If he asks, I'll tell him you went back to class."

I let go and start for the door. "Thank you, Mrs. Kelso. You're the best."

"Gigi?"

"Yeah?"

"You're not as damaged as you think you are. You help those that need it. Bad people only care about themselves."

I give her a tight-lipped smile.

The damage runs deep under the surface. A jackhammer wouldn't even scratch it.

CHAPTER 31

𝓜 agical Backfires

WHEN GRAM SEES Ryan carrying Lizzie down our front path, she backs into the house as if Lizzie's a demon instead of a girl. "What happened to her?" she gasps.

She's far too shocked to probe into my mind at this point, but I block myself off anyway. Scott and I joined as a team in Donahue's office. Scott was more concerned about protecting me than trying to figure out what really happened, and I'm not telling Gram either. Not like this. Not ever.

I rest my hand on Ryan. "Set her on the sofa."

He cradles her to his chest, breathing in her hair. It smells like the wild lilacs that grow outside her window in the springtime. He cherishes her as much as I do. She will always be safe with him nearby.

"Gram, we need your special tea."

Gram squeezes my arm. "Gigi, I need to know what happened."

"She needs your tea. Now."

I race to the kitchen because Gram isn't doing what she's supposed to do. I fill the tea kettle and flick on the front burner before she catches up to me.

"Gigi," she says, grabbing both my arms and digging her nails in. "You need to tell me what's going on."

Her attack catches me off guard. I almost let her in before I cut off my thoughts.

"Gram, she needs your tea." I try to shrug her off, but she won't let go. She's surprisingly strong for her old age.

"The tea blend is for you. It won't do Lizzie any good."

"Of course it will help Lizzie. It always makes me feel better." I jerk away and grab the tea blend jar from the counter. I measure out a serving and put it in the tea strainer. The tea kettle starts whistling its siren call. I reach for it.

"Gigi," she says grabbing my arms again. "If you use it, you could kill her."

"Gram, what are you talking about?"

Footsteps pound down the hall. "Hurry," Ryan yells, "I'm losing her. I'm losing her." He dashes back into the living room.

Gram stares at me. Her arms pinning me in place.

"Magic. I did magic." The flames erupt in my throat. "The curse backfired."

GRAM WORKED on Lizzie for hours. She had Ryan chop wood and make a fire. She sent Scott to our attic for candles. As soon as he returned she asked him to pick up some of his dad's books from his house. She sent me out three times for different herbs that were in the greenhouse or in one of the gardens, but only if Scott was back. I think she was afraid to be alone with Lizzie. During my first trip to the garden, I buried the winking eyeball pendant into the base of a lavender plant. Since lavender is calming, I figured that maybe it could neutralize any of the bad mojo coming from the eyeball.

When we weren't running around gathering items for Gram, Ryan and I held Lizzie's hands. There had to be enough love in the room to rid her of any sickness she might have, but it still took Gram far longer than I figured it would to heal her.

Thankfully, Breas didn't come home after school. Not that I'm surprised or thought he'd help us. He'd be more in the way than anything else. But honestly, I thought he'd stop in if nothing else but to check in on me (because he's so damn nosy and obsessive) and maybe even apologize about his little psychotic episode last night at Radley Pond. I mean what was *that*?

My gut instinct proved correct—he's not to be trusted. He knew that Lizzie tried to curse him the other day. He doesn't need to know about the missing spell book. He doesn't need to know about the spell book period. Or what Lizzie tried to do to Kensey. Or basically anything at all. He can disappear, never to return, for all I care.

As for the missing Kensey? With any luck, she evaporated into thin air.

When Lizzie finally comes to, I cradle her feet in my lap, Ryan sits on the floor next to her holding her hand, and Sphinx perches on the back of the sofa watching over her.

Gram shuffles in with another cup of tea she's blended just for Lizzie. I need to ask her what's in mine that would kill her.

"Here, Lizzie, drink this."

Ryan releases her hand so she can drink, but he doesn't go

far. "Do you need anything? Are you good? Do you need to go home? I can take you home."

She glances at me. She and I both know that Ryan can't take her home, especially not in her present state. I don't even want to imagine what her parents' reaction would be.

"Hey, Ryan, could you help me with my chemistry homework?"

"Now? Can't Scott help you?" he says, but there's a lot more he's not saying. Like why am I asking for help with chemistry when I don't even care about school? And mainly, Lizzie is all that matters.

Of course I agree with him one hundred percent, but I can't tell him that. I can't tell him I know exactly what he's thinking.

"Scott? He's terrible at chemistry." Fireworks explode in my throat. Scott is actually a freak of nature when it comes to chemistry.

Please don't kill me, Scott.

You're lucky Gram's here.

Yeah, there's that whole talking in my head thing. That's going to take some time to get used to, but at least Scott's willing to lie for me. Well, for Lizzie.

"Ryan, it's true. I suck at chemistry. Besides, I need to pick up some goat cheese for Gram. Lizzie, would you mind if I drove you home?"

She smiles gratefully at him. "Sure, that would be great."

Ryan shoves his hands in his pockets. "I don't know …"

"Ryan, I'm fine. Scott can take me, and you can help Gigi."

He reaches down to cup Lizzie's hand between his. "Are you sure? Are you sure you're feeling okay?"

She blushes. "I'm feeling much better. Gram worked her magic on me."

Gram pulls her lips in. I try to get a read on her thoughts, but she closes herself off.

Scott approaches the sofa. "Ready to go?"

As Ryan helps her stand, she wobbles to her feet. He guides her to the door with Scott on the other side. She seems perfectly fine now. Even her thoughts are clear—she wishes Ryan could take her home. She wishes her parents could like him as much as she does.

Gram looks over at me. She doesn't need to say a word either verbally or mentally. Her message is clear: We need to talk.

I set my jaw. No one will know the truth. No one will know what happened in the attic or what happened to Kensey. Actually, I don't even know that myself. All I know is that I will do everything within my power to keep Lizzie safe.

CHAPTER 32

Frozen Pigskin

EVERY FRIDAY NIGHT from September through November, the residents of Vernal Falls shed their conservative suits and ties, restrictive machinist coveralls, housecoats, and fake pearls in exchange for Vernal Falls High School football jerseys (available for purchase at the ticket booth). They carry pom-poms and noisemakers (also available at the ticket booth) and paint their faces blue and gold (not available at the ticket booth, but your closest neighbor would be more than happy to share theirs with you).

And if their clothing choice, cheering, and frantic sit-stand motions aren't problematic enough, the singular focus of their minds—the excitement of a tackle, the disappointment at a missed yard, the anger at a bad call—feels like an ice pick drilling into my brain.

A bitter wind whips across the field, providing me with additional proof that Friday night football games are grossly overrated. But here I am, with Lizzie by my side. And I suppose that counts for something—at least the Scott-Ryan duo thinks so. They've lit up the turf since our arrival with touchdown after touchdown. I guess they're making up for last weekend when, according to them, they were too distracted by my absence to even complete a pass.

Scott, Ryan, and Lizzie ganged up on me in school today. They made me promise I'd come to the game and not disappear like last Friday night. To help me keep my vow, Lizzie has refused to leave my side. She even lied to her parents and told them the Bible study group was meeting early, just so I didn't escape.

So I'm freezing my ass off for the sake of my friends who are obsessed with pigskin. It's no wonder my mind drifts to last weekend. The heat from my mysterious dance partner warms me still. My gloved hand traces my lips. I felt cherished when our lips met. As opposed to the Irish ass who kissed like he was conquering something.

"Woohoo! Go, Ryan!" Lizzie shouts, squeezing my arm. "Oh my god, oh my god, look at him ... Go, Ryan! Go!" She jumps up and down, clapping and yelling. By necessity, I stand up with the rest of the crowd who are equally losing their minds over Ryan's run. He crosses the finish line or the end zone or whatever it's called, and Vernal Falls puts another six points on the board.

Lizzie bounces up and down beside me. "Did you see that? Did you see that?"

My head will explode if I don't get out of here soon, and her enthusiasm isn't helping the situation.

"Are you sure you weren't a cheerleader in a former life?"

"I'd be a cheerleader in this one if my parents would let me."

My heart plummets to my stomach. "You would?" I thought we shared something more than our longtime friendship. I thought we both hated organized clubs and sports teams, and any kind of uniformity.

"Gigi, chill. I'm not planning to try out for cheerleading—I'd just like to get into the locker room to see Ryan with his shirt off."

Relief passes through me. "I'm sure if you asked him he'd take it off for you."

"Yes, but I'm playing hard to get."

Her mind's easier to read since I stole the eyeball necklace. Physically she's made a full recovery since yesterday. Mentally, I don't know. She's no longer in possession of the blasted necklace or the spell book, but something lurks inside her. She's more argumentative and opinionated. I'm not sure if that's a residual from conjuring dark forces or from hanging out with me. In either case, it's not an improvement.

The cheerleaders flip one another into the air, shouting and chanting, to celebrate the touchdown. The pyramid is conspicuously missing its capstone. It's surprising they'd try the stunt without their fearless leader. Evidently her presence isn't as vital as she pretended it was.

Lizzie dances to the beat of the cheer. I worry again that she'd rather be cheering with them than standing with me, but her thoughts tell me she's just happy for Ryan.

"Can you believe Miss Captain-of-the-Cheerleaders missed the game? Do you think she really ran off with Breas?"

"I hold no opinion on the subject. I'd like to pretend that neither one of them ever existed, and we can continue on with our normally scheduled lives."

She feels bad about bringing up Breas and Kensey. She actually thinks I'm heartbroken over his disappearance. She doesn't know about the motorcycle ride Wednesday night or what he tried to do after. I finger the mace in my pocket. It stopped his attack. If I didn't have it, I don't know what would have happened.

She grabs my wrist. "What happened in the attic?"

"Huh?"

"The attic. What happened?"

I swallow in preparation for the lie. "Exactly what I told Donahue. I wanted to show you my new tattoo, and he caught us."

She pulls in her cheeks, pursing her lips. "I don't believe you."

I shrug. "Well, that's what happened."

She glances from side to side to make sure no one's listening, then she leans in to whisper. "Last night, I dreamt that Kensey was up there with me, and that we were doing a spell together."

It was a curse not a spell. Big difference.

"A spell? First of all, you wouldn't be casting spells with Kensey unless you fancied adding giant bows and high ponytails to your morning routine."

"What did you do with it anyway?"

It, as in the spell book. *It* vanished with Kensey.

"Gone. It belonged to Gram's friend, and he wanted it back."

I wait for the fire in my throat to build, but this time it doesn't burn like I assumed it would. Maybe the spell book did belong to Darius. It doesn't matter anymore. It's gone now.

Her attention shifts back to the game. Scott throws a long pass to Ryan, and now Ryan is sprinting for another touchdown. The fans lose their minds all over again. I stand and clap, pretending to at least be interested in my best friends' athletic pursuits, but I keep thinking about Lizzie up in the attic. She acted like she was expecting me, but it wasn't Lizzie expecting me. It was someone else. Her mind felt ancient and calculating, like she had been waiting a very long time for me.

Cold dread washes over me. I rub my hands up and down my arms. It's only the temperature that's bothering me. Nothing else. Lizzie is fine. She's standing next to me, cheering for Ryan. I should have worn another layer. It's my own damn fault.

"I'm freezing. Do you want a hot chocolate?"

She rubs her hands together. "If you wait until halftime, I'll go down with you."

"I'll get hypothermia by then. Want anything else?"

"Sugared almonds?"

Her request makes me smile. Sugared almonds are the primary reason I subject myself to Friday night football games, and she knows that.

"You got it."

She thinks about what happened to me last weekend and still wonders what knocked me out for two days. "Make sure you come back."

It kills me that I can't tell her I know what she's thinking. If I did I'd lose her friendship for sure. There's only so much baggage a friend should carry, and mine grossly tips the scales.

"I will."

Most people would take one look at the packed crowd and skip the snack stand, but I enjoy a challenge. Their game-focused hive mind provides me with plenty of opportunity to throw elbows into unsuspecting kidneys, kick errant legs out of the way, and stomp on fingers resting on the bleachers. When I finally manage to break free from the crowd, a face-painted mega-fan rushes at me with a foam finger pointed at my eyeballs. Left with no choice, I duck out of the way. My silver bullet key chain with my collection of padlock keys slips out of my front pocket.

"Psycho freak!" I yell after the retreating fan.

I pick up the key chain from the ground. I used to consider the silver bullet my good-luck charm, but it certainly hasn't given me much luck lately. I remove my glove to feel the cold, pointed metal in my palm. It grows warm with my touch. I close my eyes to ground me to the space.

I am here.

This is who I am.

When I open them, my attention shifts to the chain-link fence enclosing the football stadium. Two gold eyes stare back at me before vanishing into the darkness with a single word forming in my mind.

"Soon."

CHAPTER 33

ampfire Stories

Love at first bite. That's what it is. An aphrodisiac for the taste buds. And now that I've tried it? I will never be the same. Life will never be the same. When paired with the primal aroma of wood smoke? Irrefutably otherworldly. The mélange will long call to me, and I will answer. I will always answer.

"I can't believe you've never had s'mores before, Gi," Lizzie says, jerking me back to the campfire and reality. Flames dance in her eyes. It's a small miracle that Gram covered for her even after she discovered I was experimenting with magic. My throat still burns from the aftershocks of that lie, but I would never betray my best friend. Never.

"What can I say? I've lived a sheltered life."

"Yeah right," Scott says.

"What's that supposed to mean?" I should have known he'd argue with me. He's been picking more fights than usual because he suspects I'm not telling him the truth about what happened in the school attic. Which I'm not, but he doesn't need to be a dick about it. He's gotten worse since the rumors started that Kensey and Breas skipped town on his motorcycle.

"Gi, we all know your gram," Scott says, "and while I love her, she is one wacky chick, and you've done more ..." I raise a clenched fist, "experimenting than anyone I know."

"I'm sorry we're not lame-asses like your dad."

"My dad isn't a lame-ass."

The three of us stare at him in amused disagreement.

"The bow ties, the penny loafers, the corduroy blazer with the patches on the elbows. Scott," Ryan says, "your dad is a lame-ass."

"Well, at least he leaves the house once in a while."

"Gram's eighty-two years old!"

He nods his head like one of those freaking bobbleheads. "She's one of the healthiest inhabitants in Vernal Falls, probably in all of Pennsylvania. Dad says she's superstitious, and that's why she doesn't leave her property."

I growl, before I remember my words. It's always better to use words. Unless of course you're within striking distance, which I'm not. "What does your dad know about the thought process of Gram anyway?"

"Enough you two! You fight more than I do with my little sister, and she's thirteen," Ryan says.

"Really," Lizzie agrees. "You act like an old married couple."

I shoot daggers at her. Her remark is a betrayal of the lowest kind.

"He wishes," Ryan laughs.

"Oh, shut up, jerk-off! We all know you want to hook up

with Lizzie tonight," Scott says. Leave it to the dodo to point out the obvious—no wonder they're extinct.

"Can you believe Gram actually let me come tonight?" I say.

Scott pushes out his chest reminding me of a voodoo doll ready for a pin. "She knew you'd be one hundred percent safe with me."

"Safe with you? I'm the one who's always getting you out of trouble."

"Oh, don't go back to that whole 'well incident' again. I was eight. I've more than made up for it through the years. Everyone at this bonfire can agree with that fact."

"Still, if it wasn't for me, we may never have found you down in that well out at the old Smith place. Just me and my sixth sense."

"More like sick sense. Every sick, crippled, blind, and dumb animal within a hundred-mile radius shows up at your door for you to take care of," Ryan says. "You're the Pied Piper of reject pets."

"Must be why I'm friends with you."

He curls up beside Lizzie. "I walked right into that one, didn't I?"

"Seriously, Gi, how do you know what's wrong with them?" Lizzie says.

I snap my stick. "I don't know. Common sense."

Lizzie and Ryan have never brought up my pets before. The direction this conversation is going in is making me uncomfortable, but Lizzie's not ready to let it go.

"It's *way* more than that. I can't even keep a plant alive," she says.

"You overwater them. Let them dry out between waterings."

"I'm kidding, Gigi. It's a joke."

I fling the stick pieces into the fire. "It's not a very funny one."

After she left our house the other day, I dug up the eyeball pendant and reburied it deep in the woods behind my house. She'll never find it, and if I have my way, no one ever will. But the thing is, even though she's no longer possessed by whatever evil resided in the pendant, she's changed. I don't know if she'll ever return to our dear, sweet Lizzie again.

Ryan stands up, rubbing his hands together. "All right, all right, enough with the small talk, let's get to the haunting, scary reason why people have campouts. I'll go first." He winks at Lizzie. A blush blooms on her cheeks.

I know it's selfish, but it scares me that Ryan will take Lizzie away from me. I need her. She knows *me*, the *real* me —and, dare I say, loves me anyway. She's had boyfriends before, but this thing with Ryan feels different. The way they look at each other makes me realize that something lasting is in the making. Something substantial. Something I can never give her, and that's my greatest regret of all.

Ryan's tall frame looms over the flames. His green eyes twinkle in the firelight, made all the more striking against his dark skin.

"The year is 1889. The setting is our lovely Vernal Falls. Now, I know you've all heard of the Salem witch trials, but did you know our little town had its fair share of witchcraft?"

I nearly choke on my s'more as I burst out laughing. "Witches? Here? Please. Not in our boring old town." Well, except for the creepy shit that's been happening around me since I found the spell book, but that's another conversation with a lot more alcohol.

"Oh yeah? Well, you know Radley Pond?" he says.

"Of course we know it, you idiot. We passed by it to get up here," Scott says.

Ryan raises an eyebrow. "Yes, but did you know it was named after a witch?"

"Boo Radley's mom?" Scott says.

He and I burst out laughing, but Ryan and Lizzie don't join in. They wait for us to compose ourselves, because they, like most people, don't get our literary humor.

Scott gestures to him. "Sorry. Continue."

"The witch's name was Clarissa Radley. Legend has it, she possessed the ability to bring the dead back to life, cast spells on people she didn't like, and heal any sick animal that found its way to her doorstep." Ryan crouches down in front of me. "Sound like anyone we know?"

I smirk at him and do a little witchy finger wiggle.

He jumps up, winks at Lizzie, then parades around the fire. "She lived up in the mountains around here and kept to herself, but the rumors about her powers and what she was grew." His eyebrows dance around. "One day, a local farmer's son decided to pay old Clarissa a visit. He talked two friends into going up to her place with him, but when they got there, she was nowhere to be found." He mimes searching for Clarissa by bobbing his head in and out of the fire.

"The boy wanted to test her witch 'abilities,' so he set the barn on fire. In his warped mind, he figured that if she really was a witch, she'd sense the blaze and put out the flames."

"That's idiotic," Scott says.

"I didn't say he was smart. During the fire, they waited on the hillside, but Clarissa never showed up. The barn burned to the ground, and all the animals died in it." He stops moving, as if a statue. A heavy silence falls over the group. We wait for him to continue, but he doesn't. He just keeps standing there, not moving, as if under a spell.

Lizzie breaks the stillness. "What happened? Did Clarissa bring the animals back to life?"

He shakes his head. "No, only ashes were left, but three

days later the boys went completely mad. They claimed they were haunted by screaming animals. One by one, they drowned themselves in Radley Pond."

"What happened to Clarissa?" I whisper.

"At first, the farmer was furious at his son for burning down the barn and killing the old woman's animals, but after his son killed himself, he went to the local magistrate. The townspeople got together and went on an old-fashioned witch hunt with shovels and pitchforks. But Clarissa was never seen ..." he sweeps his hand over the fire, almost touching the flames, "... or heard from again." He sweeps his other hand over it.

He crouches down and creeps around the fire, peering into our faces with his eyebrows dancing. "Some say she still stalks the countryside, crying for her dead animals. Others believe she left and went back to the old country. But no one knows for sure. She could be walking these woods as we speak ... waiting ... for more ... young souls ... to drive ... *mad!*" He grabs Lizzie around the waist. She shrieks in surprise.

They fall in a tangled heap, laughing and tickling each other. As much as I hate to admit it, they are kind of perfect together.

Scott stands up. "All right, you two, break it up. I'll tell you a real ghost story. A real haunting, terrifying, afraid-to-sleep-because-the-boogie-man-is-standing-in-your-room story."

Ryan rolls his eyes. "Doubt it."

"Just you wait," he says, his body hovering over the flames.

Though not as tall as Ryan, his frame still casts an impressive shadow. I lean forward, waiting in anticipation, because Scott is a master storyteller.

Don't tell him I told you that. It'll go to his head.

"The story I'm about to tell you I overheard my dad tell one of his friends a few years ago, and I've never forgotten it. A story of the ultimate sacrifice a mother can give: her life," he says flinging his arms out to his sides as he bows.

He remains hunched over, awaiting fanfare that will never come, because we enjoy tormenting him far too much. Plus, he's like a gremlin. When you add water, he multiplies.

"Whenever you're ready, maestro," I laugh.

He returns to the standing position, shaking his head. "I don't know how I'm supposed to work under these conditions."

"Oh brother," Ryan says. "I kicked your ass before you even got started."

"Humpf," he snorts. "We'll see about that."

As much as we love messing with him, we all want to hear his story. When the only sound surrounding us is the crackling fire, he begins.

"There are many mythical beasts in Celtic folklore, from kelpies to the headless horseman to the vampire—yes, we Irish knew of the vampire long before Transylvania came along. Bram Stoker was actually an Irishman."

"Is sidenote commentary necessary?" Ryan interrupts again. "It takes the excitement out of it."

Scott releases an exasperated sigh. "Would you be quiet so I can get on with my story please?"

Ryan nods and gestures for him to continue. The two of them could go on for hours bantering back and forth, and believe me, they have.

"The tale I'm about to tell you goes back to the time when ancient people were tied closely to the Earth. They worshipped not one god but several. Monsters, fairies, and other mythical beasts roamed freely across the countryside. Many possessed the ability to decimate entire villages in one night, and they often did. The gods provided the villagers with protection, but it wasn't free. Each tribe was required to pay homage to them through harvest donation, ritual, or sacrifice. Tribes who couldn't afford the price of protection survived as best they could, but their living was tenuous. Their numbers small."

He transports us to another time but a not-so-different place. Men, women, and children covered with scraps of leather and fur sit around the fire with us.

"None of the tribes wanted to pay tribute to the gods but they saw no other way. One tribe, the Diana Moon Cult, grew especially resentful of the gods' authority over them. They were a fierce people. Cruel. Driven. Angry. In search of a solution to their dilemma, the chief went to Clayone, the tribe's shaman. Clayone suggested a visit to Derg the Red, the Celtic God of Death. The chief trusted the shaman implicitly, though he shouldn't have, for Clayone possessed a hunger for power far beyond spiritually leading his clan."

At the mere mention of the shaman's name, chills run down my spine. I huddle closer to the fire. For once, I wish that I had someone to hold me close. I'd even settle for Breas, but who knows where he is.

"On the eve of October 31, the chief and Clayone began their journey to Derg. Halfway through the voyage, Clayone killed the chief in his sleep. He proceeded to feed the remains to a pack of wolves that was following them.

"The maliciousness of the crime impressed Derg. He wanted to meet the man capable of such treacherous duplicity. For the chief was not only the tribal leader, but the shaman's brother. Derg permitted Clayone to pass into his realm and enjoy extravagant wine and sumptuous foods while Clayone entertained him with the retelling of the murder. When Clayone finished his tale, Derg asked him what he desired.

"This was the moment Clayone had patiently waited for. He dropped a wolf's hide at Derg's feet.

"'Turn me into one of these,' he said.

"The god laughed, but he was not amused. 'A wolf? You want to become a wolf? What can a wolf do except eat a few sheep? You redefined human treachery for all time just to meet with me, the God of Death, and you ask me to turn you into a wolf?'

"'An immortal wolf, my lord. An immortal wolf that can change shape whenever he wants. Kill with one clench of his jaw. Destroy an entire village in one night. Panic and terror will rule the land, and your power will grow with every tragic death. I will bring you chaos. I will bring you destruction. I will bring you death, if you grant me this one small request,' the lowly shaman promised.

"Derg thoughtfully stroked his beard. 'Your brother's death was a beautiful sacrifice.' He sat for a long time thinking, debating, deciding, until finally ... 'Immerse yourself into the River of Blessing. If you survive, your wish will be granted.'

"The water was magically enchanted to grant immortality to anyone who survived the immersion, but the immersion was excruciating. Imagine thousands of pins and needles poking into your skin while your body is wrenched into a million pieces and hot wax is poured over you," Scott said, as if he could see into our very souls and know each of our greatest fears.

"Only those most dedicated to their cause survived the immersion. Wavering for even a second brought instant death.

"But, with his purpose steadfast, Clayone entered the River of Blessing. As the water coursed through his veins, he reemerged onto the river bank, relishing the power now pulsing through his body. He laughed defiantly because he, a lowly shaman, had tricked the God of Death. He had no intention of killing anyone as a tribute to Derg. One bite from him and a trace of the River of Blessing would flow through the victim's veins, binding him to Clayone forever. He planned to create the most powerful force the Earth had ever known ... An army capable of changing shape at will ... An army that could never be destroyed and would never die ... An army of immortal werewolves."

CHAPTER 34

*A*rmies of Immortal Werewolves

THE THOUGHT of such a horror chills me to my very bone. Edging closer to the fire, I clutch my arms to my chest for warmth.

Scott continues his story.

"Returning to his people in human form, Clayone spun a tale of deceit about their chief. He told them the chief was an evil man who tried to murder him on their journey to visit Derg. Left with no choice, he was forced to kill or be killed. He told them he meditated to find a way to permanently appease the gods, and the answer came to him in the form of a wolf. The tribe quickly adopted the wolf as their totem, and slowly, he changed the entire tribe into werewolves.

"Wolf predatory instincts ran strong in his new werewolves, and humans became tempting prey. To keep them dedicated to his mission of ruling the world, Clayone lied to them. He told them human blood was deadly to a werewolf.

Since animals were plentiful, the werewolves could control their desire for human blood.

"Derg wasn't provided with a single soul as homage, and he was furious. He tried to destroy Clayone, but he soon discovered that even he, the evilest of the gods, could not undo the power of the River of Blessing once it courses through a person's veins.

"Outraged at being duped by a human, Derg went to Brigit, the Goddess of Learning, Healing, and Fertility, because she cared deeply for human life. At his begging, though not because of it, she decided to intercede on behalf of the humans and the animals she loved so much.

"First, she cast a spell making the werewolves dependent on the power of the moon. Only on the night of a full moon could one change shape. With her second spell, all werewolves, with the exception of Clayone, could be killed by a silver dagger to the heart because only a trace of the River of Blessing ran through their veins. With her intervention, the unbridled reign of the werewolf came to an end," Scott says, bowing once more.

"That's an interesting and really *long* story, Scott, but where's the scary part?" Ryan asks with a pleading look in his eye. He probably wants Lizzie to be scared stiff—all the better to kiss her with.

Scott stands taller. "I'm getting to it. You can't expect me to tell a story without a little backstory; it helps build suspense. Geez, the audience I'm forced to work with …"

"Anytime now," Lizzie says.

"As you wish. Clayone and his army terrorized the countryside every full moon, but just as Brigit predicted, the populations of wild animals dropped. So, many times, his new recruits were unable to curb their lust for blood. They discovered human blood wasn't deadly. Instead it gave them power far beyond animal blood. It became a drug to them.

Liquid crack. The werewolves went on a bloody rampage every full moon.

"During the fifteenth century in France alone, there were more than thirty thousand reported werewolf attacks. Clayone was furious. He hated Brigit's interference with his powers. Her spells were the only thing that kept him ... that keeps him ... from ruling the Earth."

"Keeps him?" Lizzie whispers, completely mesmerized by the story.

"Oh, yes, Clayone still roams the Earth turning new recruits whenever a full moon strikes. He's constantly hunting for Brigit."

I snort. "She's a goddess. What can he do? The nerve of someone to believe he could destroy a goddess is pure hubris."

"Miss Academia, how do you know these ginormous words if you don't ever go to school?" Ryan says.

I chuck a stick at him, but he manages to knock it out of the way. Ryan and his damn reflexes.

"Doesn't mean I can't read. Also, doesn't mean that I don't know how to research."

"True. She spends a lot of time reading," Scott says. "And to answer your question, Gigi, Brigit is one of the only gods who chooses to take human form from time to time. The last time she reincarnated she was known as Brigit of Kildares or St. Brigit as the Catholics called her. Clayone was close to killing her then, but she disappeared. He waits for the chance when she's in human form and he can destroy her forever and remove the spells that bind him."

"How do you destroy a goddess?" Ryan says.

"When in human form, she relinquishes her immortality," Scott replies.

Lizzie whispers, "Why would she do that?"

"To reconnect with the Earth and the people. To Brigit,

it's vital to feel human life flow through her veins. Supposedly, when a god is human, he's not even aware he's a god. He thinks he's a regular Joe Schmoe. So, Ryan, you might be Zeus or Thor. Better read up on your comic book heroes," Scott says.

Ryan throws a log on the fire. "Still, I don't see why I should be scared by this?"

"I'm getting to the scary part now..."

Oh god, there's a scarier part? I'm pretty freaking scared right now. I creep so close to the fire I'm almost sitting in it.

"Many thought old Clarissa Radley was Brigit reincarnated," he says, "but as Ryan told us, she disappeared after her barn was burned to the ground. I don't know if any of you remember, but when we were young, there were rumors that werewolves had come to Vernal Falls."

I get up and scratch Scott behind the ear. "I always thought you had fleas. We need to get you a flea collar."

"Ha. Ha. There were rumors that Brigit was living here."

"A goddess among us, and no one said a word," Lizzie adds solemnly with the hint of a smirk.

"More than likely it took that long for the rumors of Clarissa to get back to the old country. Remember, a hundred and thirty years or so is nothing to someone who's immortal."

"What happened?" I'm more captivated by the story than I'm willing to admit.

"Rumors have it, some of the townspeople laid a trap in an old church out in the woods."

"Our conservative, god-fearing townspeople laid a trap for Clayone, the Original Werewolf?" I snort through my nose. Our town has a church on *every* street corner. A bar's on the opposite one, but that's beside the point. "Highly unlikely."

"No, *really*," Scott says, "there was a woman who believed

her daughter was Brigit reincarnated. When Clayone came to kill Brigit, the woman lured him away from her daughter and into a church, somehow imprisoning him for all time. The cost was her own life."

"Uh-huh, and what happened to his werewolf army?" Ryan says.

"I have no idea. Maybe the townspeople killed them all? All I know is Clayone is imprisoned, and it's in a church around here."

I jump up. "We can make our own movie like *The Blair Witch Project*. Let's go!"

Lizzie's eyes bug out. "Did you dip into the special brownies again?"

"Scared of an old wives' tale?"

"No, I don't think the Original Werewolf is trapped in a church around here. I just don't think it's safe to go sneaking around old buildings," she mutters for everyone to hear, but she's thinking about what happened to her this week and how she doesn't want to mess herself up any more than she already has.

I don't blame her, but still, an abandoned church in the middle of nowhere? That's like a horror-movie-obsessed teenager's dream come true. "Scott, where is it?"

He scratches behind his ear. Maybe he really does have fleas. That would explain a lot. "I don't know exactly. I have a rough guess of the area."

"Is it far? Could we go tonight?"

"We'll never find it in the dark. Let's wait until morning," he says.

Ryan laughs. Lizzie starts laughing with him. It's so contagious that I want to start laughing too, but I'm a little too wigged out about the whole werewolf thing, to be honest.

"Let me get this straight," Ryan says, throwing a stick at

Scott who manages to catch it and toss it in the fire. "Mr. Superstitious is willing to sneak into abandoned churches, searching for trapped, ancient werewolves?"

"Just looking for a little adrenaline rush, but you wouldn't know what that means, would you? You haven't even put your arm around Lizzie yet," he says.

Ryan slings his arm around her. She peeks up at him. He sweeps his lips down to kiss her, and the rest is a big, slobbering mess.

"Guess there are no more ghost stories tonight," I mutter under my breath.

"No, only disgusting romances." Scott sticks his finger in his mouth and pretends to vomit.

Ryan gives him the finger while still making out with Lizzie.

We roll our eyes at each other.

"We'll find the church tomorrow and still get home in time for dinner at your house."

"Black bean chili tomorrow night."

"Well in that case, after dinner. Dad is supposed to be back, so maybe I can talk him into takeout."

After a few minutes of silence—silence, that is, minus the slurping kissing sounds of two people sucking the spit from each other—I say, "Hey, Scott?"

"Yeah?"

I stare up at the last sliver of moon before it disappears for a few days. "Do you think there's really such a thing as werewolves?"

"About as much as I believe in witches, unicorns, and dragons. Some things are better left to the imagination."

After another few minutes of silence, he whispers, "Legends and myths do make life more interesting though."

"That's for sure, especially when you live in boring old Vernal Falls."

CHAPTER 35

etrayal

My finger traces the never-ending circles of a knot in a wide plank of the oak table over and over again, the spirals so familiar I can draw them in my sleep.

An inexplicable urge forces my attention upward. The bright yellow of Gram's cheerful kitchen helps ground me to the space.

Someone places a sippy cup in front of me.

"Drink, Gigi," a woman says, her voice familiar and kind. She sits down next to me. I recognize her from the old photo I found in Gram's recipe book all those years ago. I'm sure many would describe my mother as beautiful, but I only see weakness in the tears running down her face. On the other side of her, there's a toddler. He's cute, and his freckles are vaguely familiar. Before I can study him more closely, the back door bursts open. In walks a woman who looks exactly like my mom. The same clear, glacial blue eyes. The same heart-shaped lips. But she doesn't have the same white hair. Hers is black. As black as half of mine.

My mother stiffens. "Calliope, what's wrong?"

"He's coming. He knows," she says without a shred of emotion.

Someone gasps, and tension grips the room. Darius knocks his hand into the table across from me. A strange woman rests her hand on top of his to quiet him.

"Calliope, what have you done?" Uncle Mark whispers.

She turns to him, her glare filled with ice. "I'm protecting my son."

"What about my daughter?" Mom says in a quiet, strong voice. "What about the rest of us?"

Calliope, with theatrics worthy of a Golden Globe, flings herself into an empty seat next to Gram and buries her dry cheeks in her hands. Gram watches the woman with mixed emotions—fear, anger, betrayal, sympathy. Every emotion is there, but she does nothing to console her.

"When?" Mom asks.

Between sobs she whispers, "Tonight."

I watch my mother's reaction to the words—fear and then a resolve I wouldn't think possible in a drug addict.

"Lulu, no. There's got to be another way," Uncle Mark begs in the silence that follows. I feel like I've missed a crucial part of the conversation, but I only see Uncle Mark and Mom staring at each other.

"It's the only way," she says.

"We can try to fight, and then, if all else fails, we'll do it your way," he offers. A few other people around the table agree with him.

Gram reaches across the table to squeeze Mom's hand. "Lulu, it might work."

They stare into each other's eyes, silently communicating the way Gram and I do sometimes. It's upsetting to see them so intimate. I don't want to have anything in common with my mom.

Gram's friend, Mrs. Paige, crosses the room from behind me, pulling on her coat. "We've got about three hours of light before nightfall. If we're going to do this, we need to head up."

The scene quickly changes before my eyes. Mom's holding me in her arms. We're standing on some sort of island away from the water's edge. Uncle Mark's with us, along with a handful of other people including Darius and Mrs. Paige. I don't see Gram, Calliope, or the little toddler anywhere.

Genuine warmth permeates from her as my head rests against her chest. Her rich lavender scent relaxes me, lulling me into a restful sleep.

Out of nowhere, an ear-splitting, nerve-shattering howl destroys the silence of the night. An involuntary shiver rifles through my body. I bury my head in my mother's chest. A quiet confidence radiates from her. Her presence soothes me.

I lift my head up and glance around. The people who once stood with us are gone. I can vaguely make out their forms in the distance. I hear the clash of metal. The cries of pain. The inhuman growls.

People begin dropping out of the trees all around us. Their faces are covered with fur with broad snouts and scary teeth. I wonder why they have masks on. Then I remember today is Halloween. We must be at a Halloween party.

But why am I so fearful?

Looking more closely at the masked people, I realize they aren't wearing costumes. They are wolves that walk like men, and we are surrounded.

Pulling me tight to her chest, Mom whispers in my ear, "My Gigi, my love, my life." Then she kisses me on the forehead and hands me to Uncle Mark.

His eyes fill with tears. "There has to be another way."

"You know there isn't. Stay here until morning light. Then you will all *be safe," she says with a determination much like my own.*

As she steps away, an overwhelming sense of loss consumes me. She begins chanting something as she raises her hands, palms up. Stepping onto the surface of the water, she glides across the pond as she continues to chant. When she reaches the other side, she turns and blows a kiss across the water. A warm breeze reaches me, then darkness ...

"Gigi, wake up! Gi, are you okay?" a voice asks as I'm shaken back and forth. A voice I'd know anywhere.

I open my eyes to Scott staring down at me with a worried expression. Lizzie and Ryan hover behind him, looking just as worried.

I wipe the tears away. "What's wrong?"

"You were having a nightmare. You were screaming and thrashing all over the place."

I sit up. My sleeping bag is right where I crawled into it last night. I, however, am at least ten feet away with a branch sticking into my back and twigs jabbing into my legs. I stand to brush the pine needles off, trying to act nonchalant even with the tears streaming down my cheeks.

Something terrible happened to my mom, and somehow the woman, Calliope, was involved. She said, "*He's* coming. He knows." Who is "he"? And why were there werewolves? The last memory of my mom gliding across the water is the most disturbing image of all. And the most familiar. She told Uncle Mark we would *all* be safe.

Safe from what?

But I don't share any of this with my friends. I don't want to appear crazier than I already am.

"I guess the ghost stories got the best of me," I manage to choke out.

"Are you sure you're okay?" Scott says, his hands out ready to catch me. He knows me far too well.

"I'm fine. *Really.* Just a little nightmare. No big deal. I can't even remember what it was about." The burning makes it hard to speak. One day, I think I will light on fire, and that will be the end of me.

"It was probably about Scott asking you out on a date," Ryan says, his arm slung around Lizzie's neck.

And with that, the bantering continues where it left off the night before. Monsters and nightmares left where they belong.

Or at least that's what I tell myself.

CHAPTER 36

$\mathscr{S}$ilver Bullet

SCOTT CALLS IT A "CAMPER'S BREAKFAST." I call it "crap." Maybe I'm not cut out for this camping business if raw oats and chocolate-flavored liquid chalk are examples of camping cuisine.

After washing down my last gagging mouthful with some of Gram's tea, I start stuffing my sleeping bag into my backpack. "Are we still going to search for the old church, or did you all chicken out on me?"

"Oh, I'm in," Scott says. "Ryan, you in, or did your balls crawl up inside you?"

"Eww, Scott, that's a nasty picture," Lizzie says, gagging on his ball usage, though it could be the breakfast.

"I'm in. So are Smith and Wesson. We're not afraid of anything," Ryan says with a vigorous flexing session.

I roll my eyes at his testosterone display. Typically, he's a lot more imaginative.

I hold up my hand to block my view. "All right, that's enough manliness for this early in the morning."

"Morning? Try early afternoon. You slept through most of the morning," Scott says, packing up the rest of his gear.

"Really?" I glance up at the sun and see it's almost at its peak. "Guess I'm not the only one, considering the rest of you slackers didn't eat breakfast earlier."

Lizzie winks at me. "They neglected to mention that part."

I hoist on my heavy pack. "Do we have enough time to go up to the church and be home by dinner?"

"I don't know about dinner, but definitely dessert. Do you still want to go, or are you worried about Gram?"

At the mention of Gram, I remember the fear in her eyes and the look of betrayal. I will never forget it. Never. Whoever this Calliope is, she wronged my gram. I will kick her ass if I ever get the chance.

"She'll be okay. One late dinner isn't going to kill her."

Ryan grabs Lizzie's hand. "Well, let's hit it."

Fabulous. They're going to be one of *those* couples.

Scott points in the far-off distance. "The church is supposed to be at the top of that mountain."

"More like hill."

"It's a mountain, or at least the closest thing around here. It is part of the Appalachian Mountain range," he says but he can't help laughing too.

For the next few hours, we traipse through Scott's "trail," a barely visible remnant of something that, evidently, only he can see. Whenever Lizzie, Ryan, or I find a more reasonable cleared path, he condemns us for our lack of bushwhacking experience—as if the scratches, torn clothing, and grass stains didn't make that observation obvious.

It's doubtful we will find our way home period, let alone be home in time for dessert.

Finally, when I'm sure all is lost and there's not even a chance of Search and Rescue finding us, we step into an overgrown meadow teeming with wildflowers—daisies, black-eyed Susans, foxglove, bee balm, and coneflower, along with countless others. Remnants of an old post-and-rail fence mark the fields along the border to the woods.

Off to the right side of the meadow there's a scummy, overgrown pond with a cluster of boulders forming an island along the eastern shoreline. The scene reminds me of my nightmare. My breath catches in my throat, but then I release it and mark it as coincidence. All ponds look the same.

"Look, there's the church," Lizzie whispers.

I glance toward the western corner of the meadow and notice the small, white, one-story church—if that's what you want to call it. There's no steeple, no stained-glass windows, no real indication of any kind that it's a church.

"Who wants to go first?" Scott says.

I jump up and down. "Oh, me first!"

No one argues. I pull my lucky bullet key chain out of my pocket and clutch it in my hand, pointing it in front of me.

"What're you going do with that?" Ryan says.

"Nothing, spaz. It's my good-luck charm. You know that. I don't see you volunteering to go lead."

He grips Lizzie's hand. "Well, how can I compete with you and your silver bullet?"

I clutch the bullet to my chest with the tip pointing out. "All right, let's go."

Scott's lightly touching my back, followed by Ryan, with Lizzie behind him. Tension pours off them.

I turn to look at them. "What are you nervous about? It's light out, number one, and number two, the 'church' is about as big as my bedroom."

Scott nudges me forward. "Quit stalling, tough girl. Let's go."

Truth be told, the church isn't the least bit scary, but an uncomfortable pit forms in my stomach. I take a deep breath to push away my uneasiness before continuing onward. As we edge toward the church, a fleeting sense of familiarity strikes me again. There is no reason this place should be familiar to me. I've never been here before, and if I have my way, I will never come here again.

"Scott, are you sure this is the right place?"

"Fairly positive. What does it matter anyway? It's an abandoned place that is begging us to explore it."

I stop to scan the horizon. There's not any sign of civilization in the far-off distance. Not a dog, not a door slamming, not even a car engine revving. Nothing but trees, trees, and more trees.

"I can't believe people would travel this far to go to church."

"Back then, everyone traveled a long distance to go to worship. They didn't think anything of it. Besides, they probably only came once a week or once a month. No biggie. You aren't scared are you, Gigi?"

I punch him in the arm. "You should know better. I'm just making conversation."

"Ouch," he moans as I climb the rickety old porch stairs. He follows closely behind me, with Ryan and Lizzie close behind him. The rotting floorboards protest under our weight. Clutching my bullet, I push the heavy oak door open and plunge into the darkness.

CHAPTER 37

*S*pinning out of Control

THE OPENING CASTS a ray of light into the small room. Thick layers of dust and debris cover the floor. Cobwebs hang from the collapsed ceiling. The place is in total shambles. No one has entered the building for a very long time.

On the back wall, there's an old calendar. Scott shines his flashlight on it. "The calendar hasn't changed for fifteen years," he says, still holding onto my back.

Ryan and Lizzie giggle behind him. Every romantic interaction and remark feels like both a searing pain plunged into my back and a shot of warmth to my heart.

Yes. I am one major contradiction after another.

A creak. A rip. Then the ceiling collapses down on us. A scream erupts from my lungs as I turn to run out the door. I crash into Scott, and we're both sent spiraling to the floor. A giant cobweb covers my face as I claw my way out of the room. Then I hear it—laughter. And not just any laughter. Ryan's laughter, followed by quiet giggles from Lizzie.

Scott stands up and shakes the crap out of his hair. "You bastard!"

Ryan doubles over laughing with Lizzie clutching her stomach beside him.

There's nothing funny about what happened. Nothing at all. I stomp over. He straightens at my approach. I glare at him. He attempts to swallow, but his smile still covers his face. I jab him in the stomach as hard as I can.

"Holy shit, Gigi! Where's your sense of humor?"

Lizzie steps in front of him. "Are you okay? Did she hurt you?"

"Is he okay? That idiot could've killed us!"

She turns to me, Ryan still cradled in her arms. He's really working the injured warrior angle if you ask me.

"Don't be so dramatic. He was just being funny. You and Scott looked so spooked when you walked in here. He just wanted to lighten the mood. We're supposed to be having fun, remember?"

I fling my arms out in the air to reveal my wretched, filthy self. "Fun? You call this fun?"

"We'll look back on this day and laugh hysterically," Ryan says. "You'll see."

"I think the only part of the day I'll laugh at is when Gigi punched you in the stomach and your face scrunched to half its size!" Scott says.

"Your face was pretty funny." I mimic Ryan rubbing his stomach.

"No, no, it was more like this," Scott says, imitating him.

Ryan straightens himself. "All right, all right, we get the idea. All business from now on."

He acts like we made an impression on him. Fortunately

for us, we know better. Next opportunity to mess with us, he'll take it.

Lizzie heads down a hallway with markings on it. She traces her fingers along the wall. "Take a look at this. These look like anarchy symbols."

Ryan puts his arm around her. "I betcha devil worshippers came up here."

The walls are covered with all sorts of bizarre markings and undecipherable inscriptions. None of us says a word as we follow them down the long hallway to a large, white, circular room with a high cathedral ceiling. Specks of dust sparkle in the air from the narrow beams of sunlight filtering in through the cracks.

"You won't be able to pull down the ceiling in here, Ryan." I try to sound pissed off, but I probably don't succeed because this place has me awed and creeped out at the same time. The huge room is completely empty. Not an altar. Not a pew.

"Look at the floor," Scott whispers. "Now that's spooky."

Red lines cover the floor with entire sections shaded white or black. Upon reaching the center of the room, I begin following the design on the floor. The pattern mesmerizes me. Slowly, without realizing it, without thinking about it, I spin three times in a clockwise direction.

"I think we should get out of here," Scott says quietly. He starts backing out of the circle. "We shouldn't be here."

"Chicken, Scott?" Ryan teases, still holding Lizzie's hand off to one side.

"No ... this ... place ... I don't like the feel of it. Something ... something isn't right here," he whispers, still staring at the floor.

"You know what? This is ... this is a pentagram ... with a circle around it." I begin twirling in the opposite direction, completely mesmerized by the pattern on the floor.

"Gigi, stop!" Scott yells as I make my third rotation.

Before I can ask why, the room rumbles. Floorboards moan complaints of being stretched and pulled—moved in ways they haven't been since their harvest. It is a gentle wakening, but an awakening nonetheless. I try to get my bearings. Scott is my anchor. Lizzie is my lifeboat. I can't find either one of them, not fast enough anyway. Not before the floor explodes upward, shooting timbers and wood stakes high into the air. The deadly fragments smash against the ceiling. It is a battle of might and power and force. Heaves and insults batter the timber-framed roof, but in the end, gravity wins with one mighty swipe. The debris crashes down around me and falls through the space where it once lay. I alone am left on an island of wood. A movement in any direction on my part will send me spiraling to an unknown hell.

Laughter—hysterical laughter—fills the room, soon followed by horrible screaming. A scream of loss and pain and imminent death. For just a moment I think Ryan's playing another one of his stupid jokes on us, but then my brain catches up with my sight—Ryan and Lizzie crashed through the floor. But then, who is that laughing?

Peering down into the darkness, I am terrified by what I might find, but I can't see anything in the dark space. I can only hear the terrible laughter and the screaming. That screaming I'd know anywhere. That screaming belongs to Lizzie.

"Gigi, jump!" Scott yells.

I stare over at him and feel a nanosecond of relief. He's okay. He's safe. But he's on the other side of the room, and there's no floor between us.

"It's too far to jump!"

Scott looks wildly around. He grabs a rope anchored to the wall. The remainder of it is strung up around one of the ceiling rafters. He quickly unties it and yanks down on it as hard as he can. "Catch!" he shouts as he tosses one end over to me.

I manage to wrap my fingers around it, but no way, no how, am I using it to jump to him. "Are you nuts?"

Then the screaming stops. Real panic leaps in.

"Gigi, you have to trust me. The rope will hold. Now jump," he says again.

We lock eyes, and a feeling of complete trust rushes through me. Grabbing hold of the rope, I take a deep breath and leap. An all-consuming terror grips me as I swing across the void. There's more screaming, but I'm unsure if it's me or someone else. The mocking, sinister laughter echoes all around me.

"Let go!" he says, bringing me back to the moment.

Before I can think about my decision, I let go. He catches me and rushes out of the room.

Before we make it back to the first room, I return to my senses. "Wait!"

He ignores me as he runs toward the front door.

"Wait!" I yell again and buck against his clutch hold.

"Gigi, I have to get you out of here!" He shrieks. His terror matches my own.

"No, we have to go back and get Lizzie and Ryan."

"Are you crazy? That laughing thing got them. They fell through the floor. *I need* to get *you* out of here!"

"We have to try and save them."

Before he can disagree, I break free from his grip and sprint back down the hallway toward the screams and the laughter. I'm fairly certain I've gone completely insane, but the driving need to find Lizzie is the only thing keeping me going. I catch the rope I used to swing across. I yank. I pull. I need it to get Lizzie.

"Here, let me do it," Scott says, coming up behind me. He

takes out a knife, but it's not your regular Scout-issued pocketknife. It's a silver dagger. He slices through the rope with ease. "Now what?"

"Ryan! Lizzie! Can you hear me?" I shriek into the abyss. The screaming has stopped, leaving only the laughter to consume the room. "Lizzie! Ryan!"

The laughter stops too.

"I'm down here," Ryan moans. He doesn't sound as far away as I thought he was.

"Do you see Lizzie?"

"She's right next to me."

I try not to think about why Lizzie hasn't said anything or why I can't hear the comforting whimpering she does when she's scared.

"Can you lift her?"

"I'll try."

The wait is unbearable. There is too much silence in a room that was filled with too much noise just seconds ago.

Ryan groans. Suddenly, Lizzie rises up into the darkness, her neck covered in blood. Her eyes are closed, and she's not conscious.

"Scott, grab my legs," I tell him as I lie down on the floor. "Lizzie, Lizzie, can you reach for me?" I beg, but she doesn't answer. She doesn't say or do anything. I don't even think she's breathing. I shimmy forward, thrust myself down, and grab her hands. Her cold, clammy hands. "Scott, pull!" I order.

Slowly we inch her up and onto the floor. Once on the floor, she remains in a lifeless heap. Blood seeps from her neck. I need to stop it, but we need to get Ryan. I clench my teeth. Then I yell down to Ryan, "We have a rope. We're sending it down. Wrap it around your waist."

My eyes scan the room as I wait for Ryan to yell up to us. Finally, after an eternity, he says, "Ready."

Scott and I stand and try pulling him up. He is much, much heavier than Lizzie. I glance back at Scott in an "oh-shit" moment.

"We can do this," he grunts through clenched teeth.

As I turn back, Ryan screams in pain. Adrenaline shoots through us, and we fall backward. Ryan's hands crawl greedily across the floor, looking for something to hold onto. Abandoning the rope, I help pull him out the rest of the way. Blood drains from a wound on his neck too, but he's alert.

"Oh, thank god," I sigh when Ryan is completely in the hallway with us.

"No, thank *you*!" something mocks, before cackling again.

My stomach lurches, and I think I'm going to vomit, but I manage to grab Ryan's hand as Scott picks up Lizzie's lifeless body, and we run for our lives.

CHAPTER 38

lood Sport

PURE ADRENALINE SHOOTS us out of the church and into the yard. Terrifying laughter follows us. Mocks us. Spurs us to greater speeds. Our singular focus is escape. Somehow, we manage to find our path from earlier. We stumble down it. The wildness of the trail pales in comparison to whatever beast I awakened. Ryan staggers beside me. Scott stays one step behind with Lizzie in his arms. I am the sole leader of our deranged group. It's a mistake. I can't shoulder this responsibility. There's not a god I could pray to that will get us home safely.

Ryan will bleed out from the gaping wound on his neck if it's not plugged up soon. And Lizzie hasn't gained consciousness—that's a long time for her to go without oxygen. We can't keep tearing down the mountain without taking care of them, even if there's a monster chasing us. I need to try to help them.

"Stop. We have to stop," I beg, trying to catch my breath.

Without argument, Ryan collapses to the ground. Scott eases Lizzie onto a soft bed of pines needles and leaves. No one would guess how exhausted he is. He doesn't reveal it in his movements—he'd smash through a concrete wall and burst his own heart to save us—but I can see it in his eyes.

The wound on Ryan's neck reminds me of a bite mark, but I can't make sense of it. Without thinking, I grab some nearby yarrow, meadowsweet, and mullein, wring them back and forth in order to bruise them, then dab the wound with them. When completely covered, I reach for some comfrey, hawthorn, and something else I don't know the name of and clump it on his neck before covering it with my bandana. I know Lizzie needs me more than Ryan does, but Ryan I can fix. With Lizzie—well, with her I don't want to acknowledge what I already suspect.

"What was that thing?" Scott manages to ask between gasps.

Thing. It was more than a thing. It was a living, breathing thing. A thing that bit Ryan and did much worse to Lizzie.

"I don't know. I didn't see it." I turn my focus to my Lizzie. It's time to face the reality of what that monster did to her.

She's not breathing, and I can't find a pulse, but I begin CPR anyway.

Scott wheezes beside me. "What are we going to do?"

Talking while I give Lizzie compressions steadies me. "Ryan will be fine, but he's going to need a hospital, and soon."

I fail to mention the wrenching feeling in my gut that Ryan is not fine. That he is far from fine. That we are all far from fine. That we will never be fine again.

"Give me a minute with Lizzie." I continue the compressions, but they aren't doing anything. I should ask him to help me, but he's exhausted, and he needs his strength to carry her out of these wretched, hateful woods. I clean the wounds on her neck with the same plants I used on Ryan, then return to compressions in the hopes that maybe the healing powers of the plants will help. I work on her far longer than I should, given our proximity to the church and the beast I've awakened. Ryan and Scott aren't safe in these woods with it on the loose. Despite all my efforts with Lizzie, the answer will remain the same. She has the same bite mark on her neck, but she looks ... she looks empty.

"Lizzie, where's Lizzie," Ryan screams as he stumbles to get up.

The truth will not help anyone. The truth will not help me. Getting everyone out of here and away from that thing is my only priority.

I grab hold of his arms and hold him in place. "Ryan," I say, but he won't look at me, his focus is on Lizzie, *"Ryan*, we have to get Lizzie out of here and to a hospital. Are you ready to go?"

Finally, he looks in my direction, but his eyes are out of focus. He seems wild—feral even. Panic does that. Suddenly, his pupils shift back into position.

"Yeah, yeah, let's go."

"Scott?"

He comes over and lifts Lizzie. Our eyes lock, and another moment of silent understanding passes between us. He already knows the answer. I shielded him from nothing. But Ryan—we can keep the truth from him.

I grab his hand, and we start moving again, but the sun has set, and there's no moon to guide us. Branches and limbs tear at our clothing. They do their best to restrain us. To keep us in the same woods as the beast. We stumble blindly. We pray to any god to help us get out.

We keep moving. It is all we can do.

Finally, Scott's red pickup shines like a beacon in the night. I take the keys from his jacket pocket and unlock the passenger door.

"Scott, I'll drive the truck, okay?"

He nods and climbs in with Lizzie.

"Ryan, honey, you need to get into the truck too."

He doesn't move. He stares at Lizzie cradled in Scott's arms. He knows, but he refuses to admit it. He'll fight for her until the bitter end. I guide him into the truck and lock the door behind him.

Once I climb into the driver's side and lock my own door, I put the key into the ignition. The ferocious roar of the engine is a soothing, dependable sound. Finally, I feel I can exhale. We're safe now.

Oh, how wrong a person can be.

CHAPTER 39

*E*xhalations and Not-So Fairy Tales

HOURS LATER, Scott and I sleepwalk down the cobblestone path to Gram's house. As I reach for the front door, it swings open. Uncle Mark stands at the doorway with Gram beside him.

"Where have you two been?" he says with uncharacteristic force, but as soon as he sees our faces, his demeanor changes. "What happened?"

My eyes well up. My legs go weak. The shock of the day finally catches up to me. I collapse to the ground consumed by grief. Uncle Mark gathers me up in his arms and carries me into the house.

An eternity later, I find myself wrapped in warm quilts on the sofa. Gram's wiping my forehead. Uncle Mark and Scott kneel on the floor beside me.

"Gigi, drink this," she says.

The tea is bitter but familiar. I need familiar. After only a few sips, my energy force returns. Gram assesses me for a moment, then nods at Uncle Mark.

"Now, you need to tell us everything that happened. Scott has refused to say a word until you were coherent."

Staring up into Scott's green eyes, I find the reassurance I need to begin telling them our tale of horror about the day that has irrevocably changed our lives forever.

They listen with their entire being. They occasionally glance at one another but never interrupt me as I share with them every detail of the campfire and the day that followed it. I describe the meadow, the church, and Ryan's shenanigans with the ceiling before I get too choked up to continue.

"Gigi, you must get a hold of yourself and tell us everything," she says, holding me in her arms. Her touch is gentle, but her words are a command.

Uncle Mark places his hand over mine. "You're safe now, but we must know everything, every detail."

I describe the large room and tell them how Scott warned us to leave because he didn't like the feel of the place. Uncle Mark and Gram glance over at him before turning their attention back to me. I give a detailed description of the floor —every line, every curve, every marking.

I'm about to tell them how the floor dropped out when Scott interrupts. "No, Gigi, not yet. Tell them how you moved in a circle."

I don't see why it matters, but Gram and Uncle Mark insisted on every detail. "As I studied the floor, I twirled in a circle. When I realized what it was, I changed direction."

They both swallow, glancing at one another.

"I told her to stop—to get out of the room—but it was too late. The room exploded, and the floor dropped all around her," Scott says. "Lizzie and Ryan crashed down to the basement or whatever it was. Everyone was screaming, and there was laughter—hideous laughter—that shot right through you." He stops. His body convulses. Gram puts another blanket on him and rubs his shoulders.

"How many times did you turn in a circle?" Uncle Mark asks.

"I don't know. I can't remember," I whisper. Tears threaten to surface.

He squeezes my hand. "Could it have been three times?"

I try to remember, but the laughter comes rushing back to me, extinguishing any memory of anything else.

"Maybe," Scott answers for me. "Yes, I think she did turn three times in each direction, and then the room rumbled, and the entire floor collapsed except for the center where Gigi stood. She alone was untouched."

"Scott threw me a rope, and I leapt across the room to him," I whisper. "We yelled for Ryan and Lizzie, but only Ryan answered. He lifted Lizzie up, and we pulled her the rest of the way out, but she was already …" I can't go on. Tears stream down my cheeks.

"Gigi, Gi," Gram says, sitting with me again, "you must continue telling us what happened."

I take a deep breath. I am beyond numb. Beyond caring. "We threw the rope down to Ryan and tried to pull him up, but he was so heavy, and that awful laughter filled the entire room. Suddenly, he screamed, and we were able to yank him up. There was blood everywhere and terrible laughter. We ran as fast as we could out of the church and into the woods. We kept running, but Scott was holding Lizzie, and Ryan's neck was oozing blood … We stopped so I could take care of him. I worked on Ryan, then Lizzie, but there was nothing I could do," I sob, then swallow to compose myself. "Scott and I managed to get us to his truck. We've been at the hospital with Lizzie's and Ryan's parents. I'm sorry we didn't call. We were just so focused on them."

Gram strokes my hair. "What was wrong with Ryan?"

"He had a bite or something on his neck. I grabbed some plants to clean the wound and stop the bleeding."

"What plants?"

"I'm not sure. Comfrey, yarrow, hawthorn, mullein, and meadowsweet, I think. A few others I don't remember the names of. Ones you've told me about."

"I've never told you about those herbs," she whispers. I shrug, not seeing the big deal.

Uncle Mark sits beside Scott. "Where is Ryan now?"

"He's at the hospital. He'll probably be there a couple days. He lost a lot of blood," Scott says.

A silence settles in the room. A heavy, weighty silence. A suffocating silence.

Finally, Scott asks, "Dad, what was that thing?"

Uncle Mark's face darkens.

"Clayone."

CHAPTER 40

*L*ies and Prophecies

REALITY. Fantasy. Sometimes it's difficult to tell what's real and what's imaginary. My last thought before falling asleep—scratch that—before passing out was, *What have I done?* How could I unleash Clayone, the Original Werewolf? Scott told us a legend, a myth, a story, something made up. Not something based on the truth. Not something based on fact. I didn't unleash one of the deadliest beasts of all time. It can't be true. I had a nightmare, an extremely realistic cautionary tale of what could happen if you sneak into places you don't belong. Merely a symptom of an overactive imagination. Lizzie isn't dead ... Ryan isn't in the hospital ... but then, why am I sleeping on one sofa and Scott's on the other? Why is Uncle Mark sitting with me, and where's Gram? I must be dreaming. I'll just close my eyes and go back to sleep. Things will make sense in the morning.

As I drift back into unconsciousness, the front door creaks open before closing. But it's not the closing door that fully awakens me, it's the clicking of the lock. In all my years, we have never locked the front door. I don't even know if we have a key. I peek through hooded lids and see Gram removing her coat. Again, I don't believe my eyes. Gram doesn't leave the property. I must be dreaming. There's got to be a logical explanation. I should probably ask, but I'm terrified of what I might learn. Terrified that what I think is a horrible nightmare is much worse than that.

"How's Ryan?" Uncle Mark whispers.

I close my eyes, pretending to be asleep.

"He was definitely bitten. I removed the wrappings to examine the wound. Between the medical care at the hospital and the herbs Gigi used, he might be all right."

"Does it work like that? I've never heard of a bite being reversed," he says.

"I don't know. But if she is who we think she is, she may have the power. Time will reveal the truth."

"Should we tell them?"

"We probably should have told them years ago. We should have told them before their little camping trip."

Uncle Mark goes to her and rests his arms on her shoulders. "We were trying to protect them. Neither one of us even thought about them going up to Radley's place or even considered the remote possibility she could undo the spell. We thought they'd be safe."

"We were wrong," Gram says. "Let's wake up Scott. Gi, you can open your eyes now."

Uncle Mark looks at me with a mixture of surprise and alarm. I don't know why. I didn't hear anything terribly alarming yet.

As Scott comes to, Gram pours us each tea. The familiar

blend settles me in a way nothing else can. Uncle Mark sits in the armchair across from us.

"Where to begin ..." he says as he contemplates the two of us. "Do I start with the most basic or do I jump straight to the complicated stuff?"

"Dad, let's start easy and see how we do?" Scott suggests.

"All right then. Gigi, Scott, you're brother and sister." The two of us stare at each other in shocked silence. We can't even mentally project our thoughts to each other.

"Excuse me?" I ask.

"I thought we were going to start off easy?" Scott says.

Uncle Mark sighs. "Your relationship *is* the easy part."

Gram adds more tea to our mugs. "Come now, you two. You've never suspected it? The way you bicker all the time? You even look alike."

We stare at each other again. Scott has auburn hair with freckles and green eyes. He's six foot one and a muscle-bound jock. I have white and black hair, pale skin, and blue eyes. I'm five feet tall, and athleticism is not a word in my vocabulary.

"I see the resemblance," Scott says.

"So, wait a second," I reply, trying to find some logic, "does that make you my dad?"

Uncle Mark glances at Gram. She nods for him to answer.

"Yes and no. That's where things start to get complicated."

"I don't understand." I may not be athletic, but I'm pretty sure I understand the basics of biology.

"Gigi, you were conceived during a ceremony to honor the Celtic Goddess Brigit."

"Okay ... and what does that mean?"

"Your mother believed you were the Goddess Brigit reincarnated, so although biologically, I am your father. Metaphysically, I'm not."

"Oh, all right. I don't see what's complicated about that. Makes perfect sense to me. You, Scott?"

He reaches over and squeezes my hand, his thoughts loud and clear. *I'll take care of this.*

"Dad, what are you talking about, and what does any of this have to do with Clayone?"

Gram stands up. "It has everything to do with him. Gigi undid a spell that her mother died casting on the church to protect her from Clayone."

"Why would Clayone be after me?"

"The werewolves' curse of imprisonment—the full moon and the silver bullet—was cast by the Goddess Brigit to protect her beloved humans from complete annihilation," Uncle Mark says. "If Clayone can destroy Brigit while she is in mortal form, the curse will be lifted, and the unbridled reign of the werewolf will begin."

Scott and I stare at them.

Uncle Mark swallows and looks at me. "Clayone believes you are the Goddess Brigit because of the prophecy ...

One of love, one of light,
Spring forth from the womb
To guard from the night.

The power to heal. The power of youth.
Their existence to all a living proof.

As immortality weighs,
One shall fall, one shall rise,
To perish from all humankind."

"Oh, well that explains everything," Scott says.

Gram wags her finger at him. "Do not mock the prophecy, boy."

"Gram, you can't honestly believe it," he says in surprise.

Gram doesn't anger easily. "Believe it? I said it, and your mom died to protect you because she believed it," she says, pointing her finger at me.

"You mean to tell me ..." I pause for a deep breath, "you believe that I am the Goddess Brigit reincarnated, that Clayone, the Original Werewolf, wants to kill me, and that my mom died to protect me?"

Gram and Uncle Mark nod in unison.

"So next you're going to tell me unicorns, fairies, and dragons exist too."

"Who am I to question the existence of magical creatures," she says.

My eyes bug out of my head. I look at Scott. He shakes his head and stares back at Gram and Uncle Mark as if seeing them for the first time.

I jump up. "You. Can. Not. Be. Serious."

She raises her hands, palms up. "Gigi, you need to calm down, honey. Listen to your heart."

"I am listening to my heart, Gram, and it's telling me the two of you have gone off the deep end. You're flipping crazy! My mom was a drug addict who abandoned me when I was a baby. You told me yourself, or did you forget you said *that* too?"

Before she can answer—before anyone can answer—I run up to my room and slam the door. I smash my face into my pillow so no one can hear my screams. I refuse to give them the satisfaction that I even remotely believe one speck of what they've told me. There's no way I can possibly believe that I am a goddess reincarnated, that I undid the spell my mom died to place, that I killed my best friend, that Uncle

Mark is my dad, and that Scott is my brother. It's too much. Too fucking much.

I refuse to believe my entire life is a lie, a complete fabrication, and to think I compounded those lies trying to fit in with my classmates? Ironically, what I thought was the truth —that my mom was impregnated during a drunken romp in the hay with some random guy and then died of a drug overdose—was not the truth at all. There was no reason to lie about my dad in the first place—I went to the father-daughter dance with him.

Why did they lie to me?

Why didn't they tell me the truth?

Why did they make me suffer every day for every minute of my entire life?

After too short a time, someone knocks at my bedroom door.

"Go away," I growl before shoving my head back into the pillow. The doorknob clicks open. I shoot an icy glare at my intruder.

"Hey, hey, hey, goddess girl! I don't want you turning me into stone or anything," Scott says as he sits on the bed beside me.

"You don't actually believe what they told us, do you?"

"I admit there's a lot of information to digest. The biggest problem I have is what if you had kissed me at the campfire the other night. I mean, then, it would be awkward."

I punch him in the arm. "Ew, like I wanted to kiss you. You wish."

He shakes his head. "Actually, I never wished it. You and I seemed like a natural pairing considering Ryan and Lizzie were getting together. They worked on me for weeks in school and stuff, but I kept telling them you were like a sister to me. Go figure."

I tear at the edge of my blanket. "You know, of everything

we learned tonight, that makes the most sense. I can't imagine someone who's not related to me driving me so crazy."

He smiles. "You're telling me."

"Knowing the truth does put a lot of things into perspective though," he says thoughtfully. "I mean, like the fact my dad is your dad, or at least on a 'biological' level. We're always here, and when we aren't, he always seems anxious. He's constantly asking how you're doing in school, what boys you're dating, or if you take drugs. I always thought it was because your mom…"

I blink back the tears. "I know. It's much easier to be mad at her for abandoning me for drugs, than to think she sacrificed her life for me because she thought I was a goddess. And then I go and mess everything up."

"You didn't mess everything up."

"Really? You don't call releasing the most evil and dangerous monster in the entire world and killing my best friend in the process completely messing things up?"

"Gi, you didn't know. There was no way anyone could have known what was going to happen."

"Scott, I did know. Remember my nightmare?"

He nods.

"I dreamt of the night my mom died. I dreamt of werewolves attacking everyone. I saw her cross the pond in front of the church, and then everything went dark. Even though I didn't see what happened next, I knew Clayone was in the church, and still I went in. I let all of you go in."

"Gi, you had a dream because I told you what I thought was a scary story. I didn't think it was true. And, regardless, you didn't know you could undo the spell. You didn't know Ryan and Lizzie would get hurt."

"Lizzie didn't get hurt, Scott. She died. I killed her."

"Gi, you need to stop saying that. You didn't kill her. Clayone did."

"Oh, that makes it so much better. Thank you *so much* for your help!"

"You're certainly not acting goddess-like right now, unless you're the Goddess of Drama and Theatrical Woe-Is-Me."

I glare at him.

"And since I'm being honest, I always thought a goddess would be taller…"

I swat at him.

He stands up and moves to the foot of my bed. "Now that I've got you almost functional, Gram and Dad want to talk to us again."

"Great. This time are they going to tell us how to get to the Wizard?"

"Oh, I already know that one. You follow the Yellow Brick Road," he laughs as he sticks out his elbow for me. I loop my arm through his and allow him to skip me downstairs as he sings, "We're off to see the Wizard, the wonderful Wizard of Oz…"

I certainly don't feel like singing and skipping, but Scott's goofball tactics get me every time. He is the perfect counterbalance to me.

Gram and Uncle Mark sit at the kitchen table examining a large piece of yellowed parchment. The edges curl up even with Gram's familiar coffee mugs set down as weights at each corner.

"See," Scott says pointing at the paper, "they *are* giving us a map to the Wizard of Oz."

I laugh, though I know I shouldn't—my best friend is dead, and I want to curl up in a ball and die with Lizzie. My light-hearted reaction immediately eases the tension in the room.

"Gigi, we know we've given you a lot to absorb tonight, but unfortunately there's no other way and there's not a lot of time," Gram says.

"I don't understand. What does time have to do with anything? Can Clayone come here?" My god, what have I done?

"No, not yet. This house is heavily protected by spells and good-old-fashioned oak," Uncle Mark says.

Scott bangs his knuckles against the table. "Oak? You mean the tree?"

Uncle Mark points to the table, the chairs, the back door. "Yes, I mean the tree. The thresholds, the doors, the window frames, all means of entrance and exit are oak wood. Oak is sacred to our beliefs. It protects us from evildoers."

"Our beliefs? Aren't we Independents?"

"Scott, come now," Gram says. "You haven't noticed we celebrate a lot more than the traditional Christian holidays? Do you think everyone in the neighborhood celebrates the solstices, the equinoxes, and the Sabbats?"

"The Sabbats? Our Sunday afternoon Steelers football worship?"

I run my finger up and down the table's grain. "My birthday, February 1; Gram's birthday, May 1; your birthday, August 1; and Halloween, October 31."

"How'd you know those were the Sabbats, Gi? More goddess voodoo?"

"No, I don't think so, but I'm right, aren't I?"

"Yes, dear, you are," Gram says. "The Sabbats are sacred to us. Imbolc, Beltane, Lughnassad, and Sanheim, or the Christianized names Candlemas, May Eve, Lammas, and Halloween. We managed to keep them hidden from you mainly because our birthdays fall on the same days. We follow an ancient Celtic earth-based belief system. Celts believe that whatever is, was, and will be. Modern followers call it 'Wicca.'"

"You mean to tell us we're witches," I say calmly. I turn to speak in confidence to Scott, "I want to be the Wicked Witch of the West. You can be the Wizard with your abnormally large head."

He winces. "Ouch, sis, that hurts."

"The two of you need to take this seriously," Uncle Mark says. "We're not talking about Hollywood witches or the witches from folklore. We're talking about people who believe in the ancient gods and goddesses. People who believe in the power of Nature to provide for them and to protect them as long as they take care of Her. The so-called witches persecuted throughout history were the medicine men and women of their day. They were familiar with the local herbs and plants and healed people. They were not flying around on brooms casting spells. They did not have green skin and warts. They looked just like you and me. They *are* you and me."

I bite my lip, contemplating his words.

"You two are from the most ancient line of Celts known as Druids. Druids were storytellers, peacemakers, and healers for thousands of years. You possess a lineage more esteemed than any royalty or power figure in office. Here, let me show you," he says, indicating for us to sit on either side of him as he pushes down the edges of the parchment. "We'll start at the bottom and work our way up. You'll notice this tree begins with Brigit, or 'Breeyit,' the more accurate pronunciation, of Kildares, Ireland. Brigit had three boys and a girl. This tree follows only the girl's line. There's never a father listed on it. Only a son. And never a son's wife or offspring."

We follow the never-ending line all the way down the

parchment until we get to Rose Brennan, my gram. Below her are two names—Calliope and Lulu.

Lulu is my mom. Calliope is the name of the woman who betrayed her.

"Gram, you had another daughter?" I ask, suddenly realizing Calliope is my aunt. Before she replies, I notice a line drawn from Calliope to Scott. Calliope was Scott's mom.

Here I thought my mom was his mom, and we were separated at birth for our protection or something, given the bizarre information Gram and Uncle Mark have shared with us so far.

"I don't understand," Scott says. "I thought you said Gigi was my sister."

"She is," Uncle Mark says, "but she's only your half sister. Your mom, Calliope, was my wife. I need to explain more about our beliefs; then maybe everything will make sense." He pauses for a moment to gather his thoughts. "In each order of Druids, there is a High

Priest and a High Priestess, who lead ceremonies for the believers. I was … I *am* the High Priest of the local Druid order."

I peek at Scott out of the corner of my eye and have a newfound respect for Uncle Mark. Maybe he isn't such a lame-ass after all.

"Lulu, Gigi's mom, was the High Priestess."

"But I thought you said Calliope, my mom, was your wife," Scott says, still trying to put the pieces together.

"She was, but she was not the High Priestess. The honor goes to the highest-ranking follower of the Goddess Brigit. The Beltane ceremony on May Eve celebrates the fertility of the land, animals, and people. Covens sometimes make an offering to the gods. In this case, the High Priest and the High Priestess invoke the spirits of the Father God, Dagda, and the Mother Goddess, Anu, to join in union using our human form." He stops talking as his cheeks begin to flush with Scott and I staring at him in confusion.

"The High Priest and the High Priestess have intercourse in front of all of the believers," Gram says.

"What?" We shriek together. I thought I had heard everything, but evidently, I had not.

"But, Dad, what about Mom?" Scott whispers, the reality of the story sinking in.

"First, I need to explain, we didn't have sex. We didn't act for our own sexual pleasure. The ceremony invites the spirits to take over our bodies, so they can share a moment of union in earthly form. It's meant to be a spiritual experience to everyone involved, including the ring of believers. It isn't some quickie in the back of a car. It's not porn. Calliope was a firm believer and was comfortable with the ceremony, or at least she said she was."

"I don't think we need to tell them every sordid detail tonight," Gram says, touching the back of our heads. "I think the children have learned more than enough for the moment."

"I think I've heard enough to last a lifetime," Scott says. "Why didn't you tell us the truth?"

Uncle Mark—or should I call him "Dad"—looks at us a long time before speaking again. "That your sister may be the Goddess Brigit reincarnated? That her mom, who's not your mom, died protecting her? That I was her father? And that we're, by modern definition, witches? The story's complicated. We didn't want the burden on you. School's hard enough with normal problems. And more than anything, we wanted to protect the two of you. We wanted to keep you safe and innocent for as long as we could. We probably should have told you earlier, but the timing never seemed right. Life was going well for both of you. For all of us. We didn't want to change anything. We had no reason to think life would change."

I bite my lip. Life *was* going well. Then I went ahead and messed it up. But something Uncle Mark said about Calliope bothers me. Gram and Uncle Mark's version of the truth doesn't add up.

"So, Gram, you really are *my* gram, my official grandmother?" Scott says.

"I've always been. I've never treated you any differently than Gigi," she says with her hand on his shoulder.

"No, you never have. I just thought it was because of my irresistible personality and charm, not because you didn't have a choice," he says sticking his lower lip out.

She tousles his hair. "Who do you think you get your irresistible personality and charm from, silly?"

I watch the two of them while I run figures in my head. Scott's birthday is August 1. My birthday is February 1—nine months after the union thing. According to my calculations, Calliope was six months pregnant with Scott when the whole union thing happened. Uncle Mark told us that she was comfortable with the ceremony … or at least she said she was.

My dream becomes clearer as nearly every aspect of it is confirmed as truth. Calliope was upset when she came bursting into the house. She said, "*He's* coming. He knows." She said she was protecting her son, but Scott was safe. She sent Clayone because she was pissed at my mom's union with Uncle Mark. I served as a constant reminder of what they did. She wanted me dead. She knew my mom would sacrifice her life for me. She killed my mom.

"Is everything all right, Gigi?" Uncle Mark murmurs, reaching out to touch my hand.

My eyes shift back into focus, and I realize we're the only ones left at the table.

I glance around. "Where did everyone go?"

"Gram sent Scott to his bedroom to sleep. She said to say 'good night,' or should I say, 'good morning,'" he says, ducking his head to peek out the window.

"Uncle Mark, can I ask you a question?"

He nods his head with effort.

"Calliope wasn't okay with the Beltane ceremony, was she?"

He shakes his head. "No, she wasn't. She believed I was in love with your mom, even though I was her husband, and she was pregnant with our child."

"Were you?" I whisper, afraid of the answer.

He swallows. "Yes."

"That's why she betrayed my mom, isn't it?"

He studies me. "How do you know about that?"

I tell him my dream from beginning to end. As I finish, we sit for a long while, neither one of us speaking. Then he stands up, kisses me on the forehead and heads to the living room.

"What happened to Scott's mom?" I whisper to his departing back.

"She drowned herself in Radley Pond," he says in a dull, lifeless tone as he steps over the threshold to the living room.

"Dad," I whisper hesitantly. He stops but doesn't turn to face me. "Do you believe I'm Brigit?"

"Yes," he replies and continues on. His footsteps sounding heavier than before.

I lie.

I cheat.

I steal.

I am not a god.

The End

Keep reading for an excerpt of
Blood Moon: The Goddess Chronicles Book Two

JOIN THE CIRCLE

Be the FIRST to find out when *Blood Moon: The Goddess Chronicles Book Two* is available for purchase. PLUS, receive Newsletter Subscriber Only Bonus Content, insight on Celtic Mythology, Druids, Witches, Werewolves, and Magic, and so much more!

Join the Circle today!

BLOOD MOON: THE GODDESS CHRONICLES BOOK TWO

K.B. ANNE

PROLOGUE

I've tempted fate one too many times not to be surprised as the killer stalks toward me, but still I am. An ocean separated us. An *ocean* for god's sake. But still he's here. Ready to rip out my throat.

CHAPTER 1

Hanging from the Gallows

MY BEST FRIEND IS DEAD. Dead. It doesn't seem possible that the world continues to rotate around the sun without her in it. It certainly isn't fair that I continue breathing while she gets shoved into a coffin and dropped into the ground.

How did I, Gigi Brennan, release Clayone, the Original Werewolf?

Oh, that's right, because Gram and Uncle Mark—or really "Dad"—believe I'm the Celtic Goddess Brigit reincarnated.

The last time I checked, goddesses don't break into their neighbors' houses, or lie to the school principal on a daily basis or, well, make out with anyone with a pulse.

Do gods and goddesses even kiss? Zeus went far beyond lip locking with mortals. Ever hear the term "demigod"? During his prime, Zeus had armies of them. But he's a Greek god. Are Celtic gods and goddesses just as horny as him?

Though, honestly, being Brigit is the least of my worries.

The moment Lizzie stopped breathing, I stopped breathing. I stopped believing in everything and everyone. The lies Gram and Uncle Mark told me confirm that the world has gone insane. That it's a world not worth living in anymore.

A world I don't want to live in anymore.

Knock. Knock.

"Gigi, honey?" Gram calls out from the other side of the door. "Some officers are here, and they'd like to speak with you and Scott about what happened up at the church."

Do I even know what happened? It feels like a bad trip, and one I don't want to repeat.

"I'm not talking to anyone," I mutter into my pillow.

The door clicks open, and she walks in. "Dear, you have to talk to them."

The mind reading stuff is really a pain in the ass, especially when it's my own grandmother reading my freaking mind.

I flip over to face away from her. "I don't want to."

The bed moves as she sits down next to me. Her presence alone calms me more than any tea or smell ever could.

"Gi, you owe it to your friends to make sure no one else goes up there and gets injured. Or worse."

I stare at the wolf statue on my nightstand. Wolves are innocent. Pure. Good. How could someone turn them into a killing machine?

"I don't even know what to tell them."

Scott's the storyteller. He's the entertainer. He's the good one.

"You will," she says.

She's always given me far too much credit. Credit I do not deserve.

"You do deserve it, Gigi. You do."

The climb down the stairs feels like I'm approaching the gallows. Not that the thought didn't already cross my mind, but Gram, Scott, and Dad shouldn't have to endure my death. The longer I live, the more I'll suffer, and I should suffer for what I've done.

When I enter the living room, Scott's leaning against the wall and Dad's standing at the door in quiet conversation with the two officers. In my heart, I know it's right to call him Dad. He's always been there for me, always watched out for me. Just like Scott. We might now officially, or at least metaphysically, be related by blood, but they have always been my people. They are my family, and I will do everything in my power to protect them.

"Gigi, Scott, this is Officer Lamberton and Officer Smith. They'd like to talk to you about what happened yesterday. Shall we?" Dad says, gesturing to the sofas. The same sofas we passed out on last night. The same sofas where we discovered the shocking truth that I unleashed the most evil werewolf of all time. A werewolf who bit Ryan and killed Lizzie. A werewolf who will kill anyone who comes near the church in order to feed. In order to gain strength. In order to kill me. I don't fear for my own life, but I fear for Gram, Scott, and Dad. I fear for these officers.

"We've already been to the hospital to talk to Ryan," Officer Smith says.

I recognize him. He's Tom's dad. Tom plays football with Scott and Ryan.

The flame of possibility blooms within me. "He's conscious?"

"He is, but he's completely delusional. His version of the events yesterday are pretty outrageous. He claims some type of beast attacked the two of them. We're hoping you two can help us figure out what we're going up against when we go up there."

I raise my hand. "That won't be necessary."

Everyone turns to me, and unfortunately, I know what they're thinking. I know what they're all thinking.

"It won't be necessary to go up to the church. There isn't anything up there."

"Gi?" Scott says. He wants to tell them everything. Every last stinking detail.

Don't.

His forehead bulges, but he keeps his mouth shut.

"We were camping in the woods Saturday night, and we were telling ghost stories. We decided to hike up to the old church the next day. When we got there, we were messing around, trying to scare each other. It was dark inside, and it was covered with cobwebs. Then all of a sudden, the floor collapsed, and Lizzie and Ryan fell down to the basement or something. Everyone was screaming. Ryan lifted Lizzie, and Scott and I pulled her up the rest of the way. Blood was everywhere."

I babble on and on, unable to stop. Knowing if I do stop, even for a breath, I won't be able to continue.

"Then we pulled Ryan up. As soon as he was out of the hole, Scott lifted Lizzie, and we ran out of the place as fast as we could. We were so scared. When we were far away from the church, we stopped. That's when I cleaned Ryan's cut and bandaged him. I tried to find a pulse on Lizzie, but she was already ... she was already ..." A wave of sobs eliminates my power of speech.

Scott wraps his arm around me, immediately calming me. "When we got them out of the woods, we drove to the hospital, but it was too late for Lizzie," he says.

"Ryan said they were attacked by some type of beast," Officer Lamberton says. "Do you know what he's talking about?"

We know exactly what he's talking about.

"The building was really old, and the floor was covered in animal droppings. A rat probably bit him when he fell."

A freaking giant rat.

I cringe at the memory of Ryan's blood-curdling scream. If someone lights a match near my mouth, I will burst into flames.

Lamberton's eyes shine as he caresses his holstered gun. "You're sure there's no rabid animal we need to hunt down?"

We nod our heads in agreement.

They buy our story hook, line, and bullshit.

Officer Smith stands up with Officer Lamberton following. "Appreciate your time. We've got everything we need. If we have more questions, we'll give you a call."

Dad shakes each of their hands. "Thank you, gentlemen."

"Ma'am," they say together, nodding at Gram before Dad closes the door behind them.

Gram wraps her arm around me. "You did great, Gigi. I knew you would."

Dad agrees with her, but there is one person in the room not in agreement.

"Why didn't you tell them the truth? Why did you lie to them? They're going to think Ryan's a complete nutjob now."

Dad crouches down in front of us. "Scott, that's enough. Gi did the right thing. If you told them what really happened, do you think they'd believe you anyway? And what would happen to them if they went up to the church?"

Before Scott can answer, Dad continues. "They would be killed. Clayone would feed on them and grow stronger with every death. Right now, he's trapped in the church until the next full moon. That evening, he will leave his prison to feed. When he builds enough strength, he will come here. The spells we have in place and the others we will cast should keep him out, but in just over a month, he will be more powerful than he has been in a thousand years."

"Why's that?" Scott asks quietly.

"On October 31, the eve of Samhain, there will be a Super Blue Blood Moon during the lunar eclipse. The strong oak doors of this house and the enchantments placed upon it may not be enough to protect any of us," Dad whispers.

Shit. What have I done?

To be continued...

JOIN THE CIRCLE! Be the FIRST to find out when *Blood Moon: The Goddess Chronicles Book Two* is available for purchase. PLUS, receive Newsletter Subscriber Only Bonus Content, insight on Celtic Mythology, Druids, Witches, Werewolves, and Magic, and so much more!

Join the Circle today!

ABOUT THE AUTHOR

KB once smashed into a tree while skiing. The accident led to a concussion, a cracked sternum, temporary notoriety as a sixth grader returned from the dead, and the realization that fictionalized accounts are way more interesting than just slipping on the ice.

Druids live among us, or at least they do in her YA series *WIDE AWAKE* debuting October 2018. When Gigi reverses the spell her mom died casting, she discovers that witches, werewolves, and magic aren't just bedtime stories. They're her story.

Join the Circle! Be the FIRST to find out about new releases from Best-Selling Author, K.B. Anne. PLUS, receive Newsletter Subscriber Only Bonus Content, insight on Celtic Mythology, Druids, Witches, Werewolves, and Magic, and so much more! Join the Circle today!

ACKNOWLEDGMENTS

Wide Awake began four years ago when I wrote what I thought was a standalone. At the first night of my first writing class at the Highlights Foundation with Harold Underdown, he said, "Oh, you're the scary story in the woods writer."

I responded, "Yes, I guess I am."

He soon followed with, "It needs to a trilogy."

Three years later, I returned to the scary story in the woods ready to tear it down and build it back into a series. Thank you Harold. *Wide Awake* is better for it.

My Middle, you are my Ideal Reader. Thanks for encouraging me to listen to the voices inside my head. I can't wait to co-write with you.

My Big, your belief in me makes me believe in myself.

My Little, Cowgirl up! Hours of riding keeps this mama happy!

Alison Green Myers, you've read more versions of *Wide Awake* than anyone I know. Thank you A. You are beautifully fierce.

Meggan Turner, you're my first official fangirl. Thank you for your continued support and your willingness to read drafts of my stories. Even quickly, terribly written chapters. You will go far!

Laura Parnum, you rolled up your sleeves and wielded your fingers with broad strokes to fix my grammar, discover inconsistencies, and appreciate my humor. (Or I least I hope you did.) Thank you Laura. Any tipos or punctu@tion errors are mine @lone.

Nif, I can never thank you enough for not laughing at me. You are my Fierce, Beautiful Friend.

Donna Boock, you always give me positivity and focus when I need it the most.

Lorraine Blough, thank you for reading early early versions of my first books. They're not called the vomit drafts for nothing. Thank you for your strong stomach.

Denna D, my mega-reader high school friend, you will always be the shit.

Sera Rivers, thank you for letting me pick your brain about Jehovah Witnesses. Lizzie rocks because of it.

Stephanie Keener, how could I forget my Twilight buddy? Thank you for reading an early version and making it a better story.

Anika Willmanns, Ravenborn Covers, when I saw your Darkest Days cover I knew that I had found Gigi's cover soulmate. Thank you for being so incredibly talented!

My Rising Starrs, present and future, thank you for joining me on this journey. My favorite Rising Starrs include Meggan, Heather, Shahna, Jade, Reilly, Gurlay, Kelsey, Carolina, Dawn, Candice, Sophie, Angie-Lee. A million thank you's! You are my Insta-friends!

Last, but certainly not least, You. Never forget that you are an amazing human being. You are unique. You are special. You are fierce. I can't wait to hear you roar!

Join the Circle! Be the FIRST to find out about new releases from Best-Selling Author, K.B. Anne. PLUS, receive Newsletter Subscriber Only Bonus Content, insight on Celtic Mythology, Druids, Witches, Werewolves, and Magic, and so much more! Join the Circle today!

Made in the USA
San Bernardino, CA
26 October 2018